Deep Overstock

#5: Dreams

June 2019

" Dreams are today's answers to tomorrow's **"** questions.

Edgar Cayce

META - DREAMS

EDITORIAL

EDITOR-IN-CHIEF: Bobby Eversmann

MANAGING EDITORS: Ariel Kusby

PROSE: Mickey Collins & Bobby Eversmann & Z.B. Wagman & Amanda Pecora & Caroline McCulloch

POETRY: Ariel Kusby

SOCIAL MEDIA: Ariel Kusby & Caroline McCulloch

WEB DESIGN: Bobby Eversmann

INTERIOR DESIGN: Mickey Collins

COVER DESIGN: Kevin Sampsell

CONTACT: deepoverstock@gmail.com
         deepoverstock.com

ON THE SHELVES

Letter from the Editors

Dearest dreamers,

When we sleep our brain does some audio-visual gymnastics to help us understand ourselves. But more often than not, our dreams don't just stop when we wake up.

We gave you a bottle of metaphorical sleepytime tea and asked you to report back. In return you gave us dreams by the pillowful. Thank you for crushing the sand from the corners of your eyes and using that to ink your nightmares for us. Reading all of your submissions kept us awake at night, in the best of ways.

In this issue you'll find desires and dreams in all shapes and sizes. We appreciate you continuing this journey through our collective minds with us.

After you finish reading this issue we would ask you to turn your attention away from the ever-changing dreamscapes that haunt us and to begin to think of another changing time in history: that of the western--a time of outlaws and sheriffs, of humans versus nature, of new technologies and strange lands.

Giddyup!

DO Editors

It Dreams

by Jonathan van Belle

For our setting, your setting: your smoothie-purple mouth, your shoelaces, every refracted ray of light, all the shifting corners along your walk (and all parenthetically interesting details). The setting, in other words, is your every sense upon every facet, layer, and opening. The setting flows—it is there and gone, there and not, moving quicker (it cannot be caught). The setting is somewhere, in time (sensed incompletely) and space (extending out indefinitely). A visual edge never appears—it is only inferred, assumed.

For our character, a reader: reading "reading" on a page, mute, and now aware of its own silence, as if waking from a musical daydream. Before now, it was only a characterless setting; now *it* is here, doubled on itself. It is a familiar presence, even too familiar (too intimate). It flows, flowing up whenever it will, to make itself knowable. Here and now *you* are (where else would you be?).

For our plot, this dream; but what connects the dream of purple to the dream of sweetness?—to the dream of a mouth? Where do they float? How do they fuse?

An interlude: it comes upon a sentence, this sentence, arranged, it says, as a line from left to right. Across, above, behind, and everywhere around the sentence, come faces (your faces) that disagree. "It reads right-to-left *to me*," says one. "To me, it's an infinite plane," says a third, traveling a beam. The second one speaks next, "I'm the first to say it: there's no right way to read it."

"To light, the earth is flat," comes the fourth soundless voice. "To you, the light is *vision*."

For our falling action, two falling objects that seem motionless to themselves: an earth, a reader. Everything is falling. Everything is still. *How odd this dream.*

For our ending, your ending, which, as absence, you will not—. It does not—. Neither setting, nor character, nor plot reveal the end. It cannot be a *now*. Shall we listen (inside) to a poem (to a dream) without a home?

We, old mirror, even we're in here

With infinity's first step.

These arms, these hands—how many?

Uncountably many (without a left and without a right).

You, painting of a face in a mirror, even you're in here,

—where "here" means only near-to-me.

It dreams.

You Okay

by Kevin Sampsell

The only thing comforting about the hour of 3am is knowing that someone who is in pain is no longer in pain, is sleeping, is breathing steady, is not thinking of the reality of life.

Someone knocking on your door at 3am is the scariest thing in the world. They ask you, advise you, recommend to you, tell you to get in an elevator with them. You walk fifteen minutes in the gray dark alongside them and they say it's "just a little further" and you walk for twenty more minutes until you come upon a door and it opens. You are even more tired now but you can't rest or even lean. It's a small elevator and there are dirty napkins everywhere and you're afraid to touch them so you have to stand close together as you feel yourself being jostled upward in that ghostly way that elevators move without you actually seeing where they're going. There are no buttons or numbers in sight, or maybe they are behind the filthy napkins.

It smells like chocolate milk in there and the sound coming from just above your head is the sound a glass of chocolate milk makes when it's being stirred.

* * *

You begin to understand that this is only part of your experience. You have another body somewhere, or actually two other bodies. One of them is likely sleeping. The other one is probably awake and angry, coughing persistently, driving a rusted Uber.

* * *

You feel your crotch buzzing and reach in to pull out your cell phone. An ex-lover who hasn't spoken to you in ten years is texting you. "Hey are you okay?" You can't remember what she looks like. You ask her to send a photo of herself.

She says, "You first," and you start to wonder if this is some kind of scam or spambot.

As you are texting, the door of the elevator opens and you realize you're alone. You walk out and see a long hallway ahead of you. There is a desk with a pile of hospital papers on it and a glass of metallic-looking water.

You pour the water on the ground and take a photo of your reflection in it. You send the photo to your ex-lover but there is no response. You start to think it was a wrong number.

Hours pass through you, slowly, one at a time. You feel them exiting your face. You wonder if you're in a coma. A cloud of gnats hovers a few feet in front of you, crying like a baby.

* * *

You have parked your Uber in front of a pink house that looks familiar. The moon spotlights it and you half-expect the house to tear from its foundation and levitate, abduction-style.

You have waited five minutes for the customer and you should drive away but you don't. It feels like magic slumber hour and no one else is awake. You could take all your clothes off and run through the streets and no one would know. You could light a mailbox on fire and it would look pretty. You could cough at the stars as loud as you want. You could smash twenty Neti pots on the sidewalk without upsetting anyone.

You could set up an easel and paint a portrait of that raccoon watching you.

* * *

Eventually, the ex-lover texts you a single word: "Look." And there is a blurred photo of a stubby arm holding a tennis racquet. You stare at it and see her face appear where the strings should be. A long neck tilting forward. You let your eyes blur more and realize you can't remember the last time you ate.

You text back: "I see."

She types back quickly, "Do I look good?"

* * *

Inside the familiar pink house is the you that is sleeping. You are having a dream that your two ex-spouses have married each other. They open a café called Spouse's. You wonder if all of this is legal. You never dream. You never drink coffee. You never use the word Spouse. You feel so heavy while trying to fathom this all that you forget who you are and how many you are.

Are you a lawyer or a bookseller?

An elevator?

A hospital bed?

* * *

You read through the hospital files and locate one with your name. It has a room number on it and you decide to go looking. The hallways seem extra wide and long. It takes you several minutes to get from room to room, so you remove your shoes. You get a running start in your socks until you're sliding. This works well, like you're on an invisible skateboard, casually glancing at the room numbers as they flash by.

When you get to the right number, there is a handwritten note with an address. It is written in pink and someone has drawn a frowny face on it.

* * *

You are drinking chocolate milk while sitting on the hood of your car. You start to feel nervous and wonder if an imposter Uber came before you and picked up your customer.

You look for your Uber rulebook but can't find one in the glove compartment. There are seven individual gloves without a match in there instead, plus a Buick owner's manual, even though your car is a Toyota.

You start to shake and cough as you approach the house. You wish you could shave all the mucous off of the walls of your throat with a butter knife. It's such a nagging feeling, wanting to hollow yourself out, to scrape your tubes clean, to breathe easy. You have a knife in your pocket but it's not for that. It's for waking up your inconsiderate customer.

* * *

You dance through wet grass in your socks. You jump and fly. You take off your belt and whip it over your head. A leather propeller, sparking at the UFO moon. You leap over houses and hurdle Hyundais.

When you find the address, you see a raccoon spying on you from the bushes. You make up a name for it (Robert) and try to coax it out. You get closer and realize it is not a real raccoon but a freshly painted portrait of one instead. The black mask on its face dripping black tears. You cell phone starts buzzing with a call from "Ex Lover" but you ignore it. You dig a hole near a bed of flowers. You bury it with your bare hands. You piss, you spit, you water the ground.

The front door of the pink house is open. When you walk inside, your knack for flying, for floating, for levitating, is grounded. The lights are off but there are slats of moonlight cutting through as you follow the sound of bed springs.

When you see the bed, there is someone sitting up in it. The person looks to be yawning but there is nothing audible coming out. Facing the person in bed is someone crouched low, as if to attack. Their mouth is O-shaped as well, and frozen in silence. Both of these people turn to look at you, synchronized like twins. A hot flash of urgency rises to the surface of your skin. You shape your mouth like theirs. You tighten your body like them. You reach up to your hair and mess it up like theirs. You try making a yawn, a scream, a word. But it's only silence that gets louder. You close your eyes and burst them open.

You close your eyes and burst them open.

You close your eyes and burst them open.

The Wet Feather
by Ryan Hall

The late autumn grass was crackling in our ears, faces lying sideways on the ground with the dry blades rubbing coarsely against our skin, as we waited quietly on the hillside. We spoke seldom, and in hushed voices, fearing any noise may off-set the chance of the event. We were watching the old house, long abandoned, perched in the dull light of the sun in an overcast sky. Our hands and lips were trembling, eyes dancing in random directions, ears pitched to the faded sound of dead leaves drifting. He had promised me a sight, but time was wearing away at my patience.

"I don't think they're coming," I said.

"Just wait," he said. "Sometimes it takes a while."

We were finally ready to leave when we heard it, a muted shriek on the horizon, small dark flecks in the distance that turned to fleeting battalions all soaring towards the structure. Rows upon rows rushed over our heads, circling in elaborate patterns before crashing into the house from all directions, tearing through windows and rotting wood. The sun, now cutting through the grey clouds, caught the shards of broken glass, casting them with a nuclear brilliance. The hollow sounds of their fragile breaking bodies sent waves of static down our spines, limbs shuddering with the collapse of their bones.

When it was over we ran to the nearly demolished house, opening its massive doors to the front room. The floor was thick with wooden splinters, piled heavy with blood and glass. The broken carcasses, some twitching, some still, littered every stretch of the old foyer and staircase. A shower of feathers still wet with impact fell gently through the air to the remains of their former owners.

"It's that time of year," he said. "Not all birds fly south."

Moneymaker

by Geoff Wallace

When the smoke cleared, I knew my essay was done. I was writing on a prairie cabin's porch. I set down my pen and poured a few drinks, then lit cigars and let them burn like candles for an hour. Satisfied, I called a friend and told him I was going to subtitle the essay "Subconscious ideas received in a dream." I picked up my pen again and drew a diagram over the essay itself, inserting extra ideas into each sentence.

There was a knock from inside the cabin. As I turned, I blinked and saw I was in bed. *That's odd*, I thought. I looked to the bedside table where my finished essay lay, a sticky note on top. I picked it up and saw a single word written there: *Metadream.*

"I should remember," I said to the room, "to write that down later."

I got out of bed in my hotel room, picked up a spare notebook, and started writing a script about a writer writing a meta-horror film. I'd seen a film like this before, but I'd added a twist: the writer took horror stories and applied them to the plots of non-horror films and TV shows that'd already been made. The writer had written a *Real World* reality TV horror film, a coming-of-age/starting-college horror film, and a Mark Wahlberg action-horror film, and he'd gotten filthy rich in the process, but now he was haunted by what he'd done to the original films.

I couldn't figure out what that haunting looked like, what shape the horror would take, but I told myself this thing would write and sell itself—I definitely had to write it all down as soon as possible. So I picked up my pen and set to writing a mock stalker's diary about other women in the building until a heavy noise from the hall startled me. Putting my notebook down, I crept over to the door, and got down on my hands and knees. I angled one eye against the floor and peered under the door's edge—some terrifying feet tromped past, and I let out a yelp. It took me a moment before I realized those were just the feet of the girls from the *Real World* horror flick filming on the

next floor down. I let out a sigh of relief, got dressed, and went
outside.

My old friend Mick was waiting there in a white Cadillac. In
the back was a fat businessman, gazing out the window. I sat
in the front with my notebook and started writing my dreams
while the businessman requested Mick play country music
laced with alpine horns. Mick nodded, fiddling with the dials,
then turned to me. "You wanna get high?" he said. I nodded
and, without turning away from the window, the businessman
handed Mick several bags of tea. Mick eyeballed the teabags
then handed two over to me, and I got out on the next street
corner that opened onto miles of empty prairie, carrying a paper sack and my journal. *This seems like as good a place as any*, I
thought, so I took the drugs and started tripping.

I found myself walking through the walls of an unfinished
cathedral. Wandering through hallways, I came to a swimming
pool and walked into the water; the drugs made it so I didn't
need to breathe. There were windows underwater and the sun
shone through them, transforming the water into different
colors. The sun inside was stuck in a sunset and the sky was a
permanent hot brick. "This is all part of the process," I said.

A man appeared above me at the water's edge; I couldn't
remember his name. He walked into the pool, looked at me,
and transformed into Spock. As he moved his limbs, he released
clouds of blood. "Go with the orcas," he said, and got out of the
pool. I got out of the pool and as soon as I toweled off the trip
ended, the strange swimming pool disappeared, and I was back
on the street.

I still had the paper sack and my journal in hand, so I went to
a forested park where kids were playing. I sat down and wrote
a page about a *Free Willy* horror movie, then decided it was
terrible. I crumpled the page up and it broke like eggshells. As
I slid the mess into the bag, I looked inside and saw all the tiny
eggshell shards were individual letters. "A puzzle," I said. "I'll
have to put that together later."

A kid came over to me. "Hey," he said, latching himself onto my arm, "play with me."

"No," I said. "I have to write down these dreams, and I can't do it when you're on my good arm." I picked up my notebook again, but as I clumsily flipped through it with my free hand, I began to notice a pattern I hadn't seen before.

Each time I'd gone to write down a dream, I was actually writing down the experience of dreaming the dream for the second time...or the third or fourth or even tenth time. I'd written down the same thing over and over and over again, forgetting important details and adding in false ones—and now the truth of each dream was distorted.

"Well hell," I said aloud, "Now I've got all this extra work. How the hell am I gonna write all this down when I wake up?"

"I don't know, mister," said the kid. "I can't move."

I looked down at the kid—his arms were made of vines.

Horrified, I pulled him off my arm, set him against a bench, and ran away.

Heroes Don't Exist

by Mike Santiago

My father painted a world that was consumed in shadow, but it was my mother who told me to stay idle by the glow of the light. I had to abide by their reasons and judgments alone. Demons reside in those shadows, but that isn't entirely true. However, it was in that darkness that I found absolute freedom, yet I lingered in it for a long time. As the years passed, my eyes adjusted, which revealed my scorched reality. What I saw, was an intangible amount of suffering rooted in the bowels of my own kin.

With an outstretched arm, I could see my father preparing to lash my mother again with an old, tattered belt. I cowered in the corner, anticipating that his gaze would soon be fixated on me. This had become a routine element in my life, yet I could not grow accustomed to it. At the age of seven, I could never rationalize or pardon my father's ill-conceived actions towards us, but I knew that his drunken stupor combined with his unrelenting anger would ignite his typical tirade.

As my mother pleaded for the beating to stop, he glared at her with such intensity and let out one final flay. At this point, droplets of blood sprayed the surrounding area. I began to weep, begging my father to stop, and he did. However, he locked on to me like a heat-seeking missile and grabbed me by my arm, raising my petrified body off the ground as I dangled several feet in the air.

"Now listen here, boy. You say a word of what happened here to anyone and you'll end up worse than this woman. Do you understand me?" shouted my drunken father.

All I could do was nod my head in agreement, for when I looked into his eyes, I could see the devil staring right back. And just like that, my father let me go as I plummeted to the cold and cracked wood floor.

"Now get to your damn room and go to sleep," he yelled.

I ran at Mach speed up the stairs, slammed the door behind

me, and catapulted myself under my covers. Even as a kid, I knew the only solace I could find was within the recesses of my dreaming mind. Because in my dreams, I could be anything and accomplish anything. A superhero, a knight, a space explorer, a pirate, or at the very least, big enough to slay the dragon that was my father. I could conjure up anything and not be a frail, hopeless child, or so I thought.

My eyes were swollen with tears as I began to drift away into sleep.

Bam... Bam... Bam...

The whack of the gavel against the hard, cold surface of the table solidified that the mysterious man sitting six rows away from the auctioneer had won the piece that was just up for bid. He bore a cold and calculating grin that was masked in a thin veil of darkness. Not to mention, the attire he wore was an all black tuxedo, which helped him blend into the dimly lit facade of the auction hall.

"Gentlemen, I implore you to prepare your bids as the next specimen up for display is the finest piece for sale today," stated the confident and conniving auctioneer.

Then, a cage slowly ascended from beneath the show floor, and I could see the stark silhouette of a woman from within. As the halogen bulbs locked its gaze onto the the steel box, the woman began weeping, the tears fell down her corset and pooled around her feet. She had auburn hair that was reminiscent of the embers of a raging flame. Her skin was pale as if its natural pigment had been washed away by her sobbing. The resemblance was uncanny, and in that moment, it became immediately apparent that it was my mother who would be the next "item" auctioned off.

I turned around and could see the man in black's grin exceeded the width of his face. He seemed pleased by what he saw, as if she was cattle ready for slaughter. I began to quiver and convulse erratically.

Once again, the gavel made a resounding sound that echoed across the hall. "Starting bid is one million pounds. Do I have any takers?" the auctioneer shouted.

The man in black raised his bidding card with little hesitation, which raised the stakes to five million pounds in less time then I could gather a breath.

"Six million!" I shouted without delay.

"Ten million!" said the man in black.

"Twelve!" I proclaimed with dread.

"30 million pounds... need I go higher?" screamed the man in black.

With a thundering roar, the gavel slammed down once more, and the auctioneer reverberated the solemn words... "Sold."

Beginning to panic, the realization that my own mother was sold to that bastard with his contorted, sly grimace began to fester and settle in. I grew uneasy and numb as each second dwindled away as two men carted her behind a velvet curtain.

"Mommy!" I bellowed at the top of my lungs.

Even in my dreams, I could not save my mother from the inebriated brute that saw little value in the family he had fostered as his own. Defenseless even in my subconscious mind, I could not escape my despair that had formed most of my childhood. The next day would be just as redundant and unfortunate as the previous 24 hours.

The next day, I expected to come home from school to another drunken whirlwind at my father's behest. I was not disappointed, as empty beer cans littered the ground, and my mother's throat was locked in his death grip. Her eyes began to roll back, and her complexion was recast to cobalt to match the fresh coat of paint on the very wall she was pinned against.

I began to flail and plead with him to let her go, but with one hand, I was tossed to the side as if I was defunct.

"You stupid son of a bitch! Do you want to be next? Get your ass to your room before I beat the skin off your back," his father screamed with a bitter stare.

My routine never changed its course. Every day was like this, and so I cried myself to sleep once more. Hoping that I could finally gather the strength to quell my father's lunacy for good.

And once again, I drifted ever so deep into my subconscious mind.

"Lycanthrope, I can hear your ghastly snarl, and I've come to exterminate your pursuit for human satiation. Come out now you dastardly fiend!" I shouted into the midst of a fog-covered wood.

This was 17th century Bavaria, a time where inconceivable monstrosities infested the shadows. However, our village was tucked away at the base of a mountain shrouded by a dense, thick forest. In these woods, a menacing and vengeful beast dwelled. The villagers knew him as the wolf man, but I knew him under a different banner: father.

As I crept through the murky forest, I could hear his piercing growls looming within my proximity, but I did not grow timid to the insufferable wailings my father made. With every step, I pushed on with absolute determination to put my father to rest, and to end his unrelenting scourge.

A bloodcurdling scream echoed through the woods, and I began to charge forward with haste. Loading a silver pellet into my flintlock, I stumbled upon a scene so macabre. Entrails were strewn across the canopy, and the lifeless body of a woman swayed from a tree. Her gashed abdomen spouted blood on to the dry, dead leaves scattered across the ground.

"Bastard... show yourself now. Father! Do you not see what you have done? Do you not know who this is that lies before me?" I howled with utter intensity.

"*Mooooooother. That bag of flesh I feasted upon was the woman that bore you,*" the wolf eerily stated.

"How dare you drag mother down with you. Your conflict is your own. You made no stride towards reversing your condition and succumbed further into your own demise. Mother was not yours to dismantle because you saw little refuge from within," I bargained.

In that moment, I raised my pistol and pulled the trigger – narrowly missing my father as he let out a distressing howl.

"Ahhhhhhhh," my father yelled from downstairs.

Upon hearing my father's scream from downstairs, I sprung out of bed ejecting myself from the sanctuary of my dream scape. What I saw next, I couldn't fathom, nor could I process as a 7-year-old child. A knife was planted firmly into my father's abdomen as he was lying on the floor, bleeding out. Droplets of blood made a trail to my mother, who was trembling with anxiety and fear in the corner. In a split second, she decided to make a bold stand to save her own life from the maniacal villain that had swore an undying oath to her.

At that age, my first inclination was to call the police as I had no other recourse. My voice began to quiver as I shouted at the 911 operator to send someone to our house. Within a matter of minutes, bright flashes of blue and red illuminated the living room windows. As tears began to trickle down my face, I opened the door to see six police officers rush in to find my father's now lifeless body strewn across the hardwood floor.

One of the officers came over to me and placed me into the backseat of his police cruiser. I could see my mother through the front door, still petrified, but her somber gaze was locked on me. She seemed speechless and in shock over the events that had just transpired.

"And was that the last time you saw your mother?" a middle-aged man holding a clipboard stated.

"It was... after that... it was one foster home to the next. The courts determined that my mother was unfit to raise me after that night. As the years went on, I kept replaying that night over and oer again. I couldn't make sense of it then, and I still can't now," I uttered with a gawk.

"Allen, I'm sorry, but that's all the time we have for today. Shall we schedule you in for the same time next week?" he commented.

"Of course, doc, I'll be here next week," I responded.

Despite fighting through the mental trenches with my therapist for months, I still felt as though my mind was a ravaged and desolate battlefield. As the years racked up, I could find little solace in what had occurred during my childhood. No matter how hard I tried to mount an insurmountable wall, I plummeted every time, and the obstacles grew greater and greater as the days dwindled. These were the lingering effects of PTSD that had sustained and satiated itself throughout my life.

At the age of 37 I knew I could no longer let the vague visions of my former self consume my conscious and subconscious mind. And still, after all these years, I used my dreams to escape. However, I no longer used my unconscious mind to seek refuge from my father; instead, I used it as a means to revisit my mother and undo the events that led up to that fateful night. It was supposed to be a means to an end. A way out of the darkness that I found freedom in for so long.

heavy breathing

Suddenly, I woke up, but my head was pounding and my gaze was hazy. When I opened my eyes, I saw that I was surrounded by padded walls. A steel door with a small metal trap was in front of me. It was in that moment I realized that I once again was succumbing to my dreams. I had lost all touch with my reality. I had ended up in an asylum due to the demons I could not conquer or quell.

"When will these damn dreams stop?" I shouted at the top of my lungs.

"They never will... They are apart of you now..." My father's voice said as his words rattled in my head.

Then, my eyes adjusted - revealing the true nature of my world so I could see.

I have a dream.
by Timothy Arliss O'Brien

The other night I had a visceral dream.

And
My banner was ten feet tall.
Enshrined upon it was God Loves Everyone.

Rainbows dropped from it, as I stood blocking evil.

For you see
Behind me

Was a banner reading: Fags Burn In Hell.

The hatred spewed from the banner and angry bigot holding it.

The name calling and void-of-love burned my ears,

Yet,
I endured through the whole parade.

Teaching others acceptance and love.

A queer nocturnal heart cry.

Because,

I have a dream!

(Tell them about the dream Tim!)

I have a dream,

That one day,
The world will have equity and acceptance, for all my queer family.

A world so full of love there is no space for homophobia.

I still have that dream.

Circus Chicken

by Ula Jankowska

In my dream, P wrote a musical about chickens kept in prison planning great escape. The show was all over the world in small but ambitious culture centres. And when it was coming to Warsaw I took all the people I knew. I was one minute late and everybody was already inside. When I wanted to enter, the ticket controller asked me to pay. I had no money. He said he can't let me in. My only idea was to tell him I knew P. He said that, in this case, I needed to wait and he left to find P. Meanwhile, the show moved to the place where I was, as it was a musical that was played all over the building. Every room was a stage. Actually, every room was a cage. Everything took place in a cage, each scene in a different cage, the actors moving, not unlike chickens, from cage to cage. The audience had to follow the actors who, again, were dressed like chickens. I was waiting for P, when suddenly I saw the actors, all ages (from 6 to 70) wearing ridiculous costumes. They were singing and dancing, doing push ups, jumping, running all over. You would think this was chaos, but actually it was very organised. These were very deliberate chickens. Finally, I saw my friends again. They too were following the chickens, singing and dancing. And then I saw P. He came straight to me and kissed me. He tasted like eggs.

The Dream About an Evil Queen

by Leanna Moxley

I'm nine years old on July 31, 1996, when I write the evil queen dream in my diary, in pink pen on a pink-lined page with a heart and a bow in the corner:

"A night or two ago I had a terrible dream. I dreamed I had gone to a terrible place where I was something like a servant girl and there was this horrible woman (she looked like a queen), and if any of the girls did the littlest thing wrong she would beat their head with a very hard stick, and send them to a laboratory kind of place where this man would use things to suck your brains out."

When I wrote this, I immortalized her. I went back, rereading, crystalised the memory. I see much more than I put on the page: the dark wood-panelled walls, the sorrowful-faced old man telling me he has no choice about sucking out my brains, the lumpen heads of the beaten girls. This dream follows me, in my scribbles and drawings, half-finished stories, general fears (23 years later, and she is still here).

Here's an even younger one that fills me with the same foreboding: Mama takes me to a white farmhouse in the middle of a wheat field and speaks to a woman in the kitchen there. They are across a tall counter, light streaming in the windows, I am small and alone, and in my bones I know it's a place of evil.

See, the thing about a bad dream is, maybe nothing much happens, but still the nasty feeling lasts all day. It washes over everything and seeps in the cracks.

Like I used to have this sick dream that came to me every fever through childhood. Starts out with a beautiful ballerina, spinning, and spinning, and spinning - but her shoes are scraping, grinding, on crumpled sandpaper. Then a giant pile of toothpicks comes rolling at me like logs. Finally, a girl with dark hair whispers to me, right in my ear, something important that makes me tingle and flush, but when I wake up it always slips away.

On the edge of waking, I try to weave each dream into a narrative I can follow. But it feels like cheating; I fill in the details and I know I'm making it up. As if the veracity of the dream's recounting is what matters here at all.

Listen y'all: this one time at camp I woke up in my bunk-bed after rest hour, got up, left the cabin, walked down the path squinting in the sun and didn't feel a thing wrong 'till I met the sinister clown in front of the bathhouse. Then I woke up for real in my bunk-bed and a night hag was sitting on my chest and I had to fight her, gasping and gasping for breath once I finally threw her off.

I try to tell it to you - but every dream is a "you had to be there" type of situation. Except those ones where our eyes won't open, where we can't run, every movement dragging - we all have those dreams, right?

Lately what gets to me is the ones where my Mama is alive again and clearly, firmly, disappointed.

There are a lot of these. Her same furrowed brow, hard tone, firm mouth (she looks like a queen).

Each time her presence shocks me. It's physical; I'm minding my own business and there she is. I walk down the hill and she's there on the porch, calling my name. I'm in my bedroom and she's at my door. Such a sinking in my stomach.

My mind seeks meaning in these - unjumbles - rejumbles. Piece the stories together and write myself, at least that's the impulse. There's a pattern here, right, do you see it? And if so, will you tell me what it is?

Sometimes days later it appears to you whole: a dream you'd forgotten, now here in full color.

See, there's her face, blocking the sun -- I'm four years old on my grandmother's carpet, looking up from my pile of blocks at the heat of her palpable anger. She looks like a queen But that one is memory, not dream, it's just polished to the same narrative shine.

Like the monkey story - for years I wasn't sure if I dreamed that. It was on the radio while I was driving with Mama the day before she died. Rain streaming down the windshield, her soothing voice as she counseled my friend's mom over her flip phone. I tuned her out and listened to two men talking about a couple who had a pet chimp that grew too much for them, so they gave him to a zoo. But on his birthday they came to visit and brought a cake. And the other monkeys went wild with jealousy and attacked the couple and ripped the husband's face off.

Years later I googled it: chimps, birthday cake, face ripped off, March 4, 2005. Sure enough, this one is true. I saved every article I could find in a folder, along with her obituary. It seemed important somehow, because the feeling lingered; it seeped in the cracks and set a tone for what followed.

Or more likely that's the way I saw it after, on the edge of waking, as I tried to piece the narrative together in my mind.

Protection

by AJD

We were walking on a road near the quarry, above Lithia
Park. I saw some deer up ahead and called back for you to take
a look. You were collecting flowers or rocks somewhere behind
and did not answer.

I approached the deer and saw that there were two of them.
Focusing a bit more intently, I noticed that the second deer was
actually a cougar, stalking the deer. I was shocked at the sight of
a cougar on the edge of town like this and didn't know what to
do. I watched for a few seconds, my body tight and tense, as the
cougar closed in on the deer.

I crouched and gestured to you, turning my torso around to
try to spot you. You were right there, in the nearby gravel and
weeds, staring past me and stock still. Suddenly, you gasped and
pointed up the hill with a sturdy stick.

As I turned back, the cougar lunged towards the deer. Just
then, a tall, thin, naked man jumped between the deer and the
cougar and tried to chase off the deer. The cougar loped after
the man, who was still running behind the deer. They crashed
through the bushes above the road, zigging and zagging and
finally toppling downward, straight towards us.

I closed my eyes and when I open them, we're outside a ranch
style house, similar to the house I grew up in, but very different from anyplace we ever lived. Large drooping trees, bushy
ferns, and a verdant garden surround the house. The chirping of
insects and frogs envelopes us.

We run inside and slam the door behind us. It is around dusk
now, whereas before it had been high noon. No time seems to
have passed, though, as our clothes are still dusty and warm
from the road and the sun. We let loose with short frantic barks
of laughter, unexpected relief at our escape. A growling and
scuffling sound at our feet cuts that short.

Our cat is wrestling with something under the dining room
table. I kneel down and see a small, bloodied squirrel, some-
what disoriented, trying to hold its attacker at bay. I grab the cat

as she makes an accurate pounce onto the squirrel.

The cat's muscles are hard and her body seems unusually dense. With some difficulty, I separate the back of the squirrel's neck from our pet's mouth. I take a newspaper from the table, slip it under the squirrel, and walk to the back door to set the thing free.

I open the door and am about to release the squirrel onto the porch when I spot the cougar pacing along a line of fruit trees by the fence. Slowly, cautiously, I turn around and go back inside, still holding the squirrel. I close the door and lock it, then call to you, who have disappeared upstairs, to close all the windows and make sure the doors are latched.

I don't see our cat so I set the squirrel down on the kitchen floor. I notice now, for the first time, that it has been totally dis-emboweled. The entrails are not even visible inside the vacant abdominal cavity, behind the shredded skin flaps. I am sort of mesmerized by this and, for the next spend ten seconds or so, I peer at it and wonder how it is even breathing, moving around.

You come down the steps from the hallway to the bedrooms, tell me that the house is secure and cross your arms. I tell you that this squirrel is going to die. We're looking at it, wonder-ing how to get rid of it, when the cougar starts scratching at the sliding glass door in the dining room.

The glass bows under its weight, so we close the curtains on it. We back into the living room, then turn together towards the sound of a custom-built cat door swinging back and forth above the couch. We catch a glimpse of two tails, one twitching orange and the other limp and gray, as they exit the house.

The cougar has stopped pawing at the glass door. You walk over and slide it open.

The cougar jumps inside.

Imagine
by Andy Anderson

You wake up in a seemingly unknown bedroom.

You don't know how you got there or why you are sleeping alone.

You are scared.

In fact you cannot remember what you ate for dinner, or even what day it is, but those are meaningless facts.

All you know and care about in the moment is that you are scared and alone.

And that's not okay.

You must find your people.

You touch your achy feet to the ground and head for the door.

You don't know the house either. Where are you? Where is your husband? Your children?

A stranger stops you right in your tracks before you reach the living room. You are pale, nearsighted and tears are wet on your face.

She says "You are okay. Your daughter is at work. She won't get home for another 3 hours. You live here with her and you are just tired and simply forgot. You are safe and loved. Go back to bed."

"Okay goodnight, sorry, I'm going to bed."

You feel like an idiot. You Are tired after all. You remember for a moment: your husband died years ago; you live with your daughter.

You go back to bed.

This happens 6 times as you doze off but finally dreams begin.

You aren't alone. You are safe.

Evening of an Alzheimer's patient. 2014

Our Lost Map

by Desmond Everest Fuller

I dreamed of a marriage. My own, I would call it except that I can't see the face of the woman I was so wrong about loving until death do us part. Rarely do years pass in my dreams, but we had been apart long enough that it felt like our fleeting union belonged to another lifetime, as though lived by strangers we might have seen passing by on the street.

She was faded in my mind to a shoulder buried in long straight black hair that frizzed if she got caught in the rain, giving her the look of a witch casting about for a broom. That's all I could conjure when she got in touch and asked to meet me for tea. Even her voice was a stranger's echo.

We met when I got roped into some stupid parlor game at a party of rich people I found myself wandering through. In dreams I'm cast into the current around me and pulled into the acts of those fanning me on with ethereal hands. So I followed the laughs and encouraging leers, and took off my shirt with several other young men, and danced before the other guests without ever grasping what was the point of the game. All the faces floated above the islands of tables, lit by buttery lamplight in the dark. I don't remember what happened, but it must have been then that she saw me, dancing with my shirt off, like a fool, swept up in someone else's parade.

Needless to say we left the stupid party together. Confidence flowed blue and bright through my stride then. In this dream I was a painter, and my paintings were selling faster than I could commit their faces to memory, and I was walking away from someone else's party in the company of someone new and beautiful. I walked beside her, and could nearly make out her face in the night going down the sidewalk lined with Camilla trees, just a soft smile in the perfumed dark beneath the streetlights.

The voice of a mother-in-law conjured out of the fog somewhere, swore this would never work, that we were too volatile for each other. Even after we smashed our world into jettisoned pieces, she didn't think we should meet up again, even after years had passed. But the woman I dreamed I married, insisted we meet again after our old car was found, pulled from the bottom of a river.

How the opaque milky brown river rendered up the bones of our old VW bus that we had driven all over the Philippines, was too unlikely to wonder at. By the time she tracked down my number, I'd nearly forgotten the density of the air, the water you could wring out of each breath we breathed together, living in that antique bus in the Philippines. But, as I knew her shoulder, the sweep of her hair, I could see the tea and milk in our little tin cups, half drunk, left on the fold-out table where we sat close beneath the warm rain racing itself to the puddling ground.

I wasn't confounded by the cacophony of circumstances, but the echoed memory of it all. I could remember how we thought living in the tropics would be the wild flare that would fix us. We thought my jealousy and her delight at random attention would simply slough off of us in the first seasonal deluge. I could remember all of this and so never doubted for a slumbering moment that this was my lived and shattered receding life; I never for a moment questioned the rippling fabric of the life around me, even as I couldn't recall her face.

She found me because someone found the bus we'd rolled into the river, and they found her. She found the map I'd made and left inside the bus so she found me again. After not speaking for years, having no reason to know one another anymore, we were once again sitting with tea and milk in a room where I could only recall her hands around the steaming mug, and her hair falling straight and beautiful between her arms.

She presented me with the tattered map where every location was a place we had gone, where every city was why we had failed, every river and road was how we'd pulled each other apart. All roads, no matter how less traveled, led to the last river where we had slid off the hill in the stampeding mud before the sweep of a monsoon. I don't remember how we got free of the bus plunging into the torrent. It's as if we didn't, like we died and those lives that we thought were ours just stopped.

Somehow, by some decree of dreams, this map of mine survived as we did. She wanted me to have it, and to give away whatever clinging threads might still hang between our hearts. On top of the map she laid two battered and faded hundred dol-

lar bills. It was, she explained, the last of my money that she had
stolen back then, out of anger, desperation and heartbreak. We
had run from each other, broke and alone, convinced we would
only drag the other farther down as we both spun away sinking
alone. She said solemnly that she had never had the strength
to spend any of it, even when she had to hitch-hike, and beg a
plane ticket home from her mother. She felt she'd owed it back
to me this whole time.

So she returned it all then, and said that she felt free for the
first time since we met. I still couldn't see her face. Just her hair
sweeping behind her in the morning light as she passed by the
windows of my apartment, her shape cutting the yellow glare,
walking away and into nothing.

Roll Under
by Geoff Wallace

Scene: An enormous rusted steel Möbius strip like Richard Serra would make.

Characters: Fourteen on the strip & two voiceovers off-stage. Also: a donut.

Movement: Everybody is on the strip in the strip just strip strip strip making love to the strip raking flesh on the strip staying true to the strip hanging off of the strip like your own skin waiting to jump ship (but it can't).

Voices: All lines are spoken normally except the Broken Man's. His lines overlap wane swell crack burst.

A note about Mel: His monologue is ad libbed and lasts as long as the actor feels Mel Gibson's career can sustain his own white-hot rage. But it always ends with the title line.

Ambient sound: A boiling fireball looming hungry & ready to engulf everybody (finally, goddammit).

MAN Are you sure you're going to eat before every preseason game?

TEEN GIRL But Dad, the karate punchbowl!

OLD MAN (admonishing) Now Joy, they don't do that in Ohio!

The Teen Boy cries for Joy and kisses her donut one last time.

TEEN BOY Oh, donut! I'm sorry. [Throws donut into the Atlantic.]

OLD MAN Windows 98...and democracy! Inoperable!

BROKEN MAN Who's Larry? Come to the telephone!

DANDY GUY Resident speaking! Ahem! What's that you say?

The jolly old autocracy needs extra bones? Ahem! You want to live forever? Crack open the bones and gulp the marrow raw!

BROKEN MAN Who's Larry? Come to the telephone!

OWL A one, a two, a three—*a three.*

BROKEN MAN Who's Larry? Come to the telephone!

COMMERCIAL How many licks does it take to get to the Tootsie roll center of liberal apologizing? The current world may never know!

Fireball intensifies.

BROKEN MAN Who's Larry? Come to the telephone!

ANNOUNCER He'll change us all for good! He's a brilliant bright shining hope! He's the motherfucking living em bodiment of total flux! He's lightweight and 100% tungsten! He's an unbreakable seven-foot astronaut! He bench presses with his dick, never sleeps and he can't pass out! And all he can do is this one weird trick that'll fix us all up—clapping hands for an audience of one! [Everyone claps their hands; hopefully someone falls.] And whenever he goes out, the people always shout, hey your gaw-damn tonsils will fall out! YA DA DA DA DA DA DA!

BROKEN MAN Who's Larry? Come to the telephone!

TRENDY WOMAN That's insulting. No, that's the whole point of it! No, the point of it is...the point of it is...the point of it is...I don't understand!

The Trendy Woman dives squirrel-like into the Atlantic, drowns for a second then swims after the donut.

BROKEN MAN Who's Larry? Come to the telephone!

MONOTONE WOMAN —and all the retired squirrels

squirreled away in the killing bag and officially killed
in the mixing bag where we mix our killing and kill our
mixing as we mix up the ink and trophies on our
collective shelf for the killed squirrels of our past and all
the squirrels killed in the worlds yet to come a badge
and a gun a badge and a gun a badge and a gun—

TEEN BOY You know somebody who could take a look at this?
[Upbeat jazz orchestra plays]

Audience sighs fake hysterical relief.

BROKEN MAN Who's Larry? Come to the telephone!

OLD MAN (triumphant) A man in bed with death falls asleep
in a wet room and has a vision of himself in the window
pane's water drops. His imaginary face smiles a big hot
smile like a big hot steel boat and a hat appears on his
imaginary head—choo choooo! —but that's not his hat...
and it never was!

PORKY PIG Th-th-th-that's all, folks!

Audience still unhinged as canned kids' laughter blares.

PORKY PIG [afraid] I-i-it's gonna go bad!

BROKEN MAN Who's Larry? Come to the telephone!

CLASSIC BRIT Bills and dollars. It all starves the figgas. Dollar
bill starboard, a life preserver lassoing figgas—!
[Orgasmic fever gestures] A face that's nothing but a
neck!

BROKEN MAN Who's Larry? Come to the—

*The Broken Man gags. The fireball's clone emerges from his
mouth. A horrendous yet happy feeling follows, like a dog eating
its own vomit. The twin fireballs will kill them all and soon. He
stares then goes cross-eyed, grins and shakes his fist.*

BROKEN MAN Tell him he owes me three grand!

MAN Larold...I love you...I love you...but I've chosen darkness!

MEL GIBSON No! No no no no no no no! The garden door is my thing, okay? No crowds, no crowns, no prints, no chat, no door, no figgas! Okay? The goddamn crown prince is my thing! Roll under!

Mel ad libs until he's spent, climbs off the strip and yells his final phrase until the curtain falls, concussing him.

END.

The Wraith

by Nicholas Yandell

Awake
To a dream
That walks like me
Holds my reflection
But speaks unsteadily

Hollowed
By open air
Through windowless holes
Of ghost town shacks

A phantom
    Abandoned
        Still drifting
            And mapping

                Invisible pinpoints

                    To steady ticks
                        Of some other clock
                          Under the glare
                            Of some other sun

                    Striving
              In vain
Grafting creatures underfoot

                  Rejected

                    Like a failed organ transplant

Banished

From its warm blood sanctuary

Surfacing
To sputter
The wilderness
Of wandering
The floating highways
Sinking trails
And vanishing tracks

Carrying
No option but retreat
Through dark curtains of follicles

And wire meshes of veins

The backbreaking calluses
Painfully
Gradually
Flaking away

To specks of a scar
Concealed
From waking eyes

Existing

Persisting

As a dormant key
In the stirs of sleep
Of a restless faraway being.

Shadows Doth Make Bright

by Ryan Shane Lopez

The restraints snap taut, stopping me from springing out of the "coffin" like a jack-in-the-box and forcing my eyes to pop open.

Gasping, I float a hand to the cortex jack at the base of my cranium. The hook-up is barely attached--a millimeter farther would have spelled cerebral catastrophe. The quarter-inch cable clicks back into place, sending a nerve tremor rippling down my spine. I ease myself against the tattered padding. I don't remember how I died this time, but for now I don't care. I prefer to savor these last moments of panic before the doldrum of reality forces my body back into equilibrium.

I should strap in tighter, but the slightest external pressure can result in a "bumpy ride"--anything from a snug waistband to a rogue cowboy dragging you behind his horse halfway across Arizona. The less distracted the body, the freer the mind. I've heard some higher-end models even use float tanks. Such luxuries have no place on a colossal scrap heap like the *Venture*, but still, our 154 machines, though outdated, poorly-maintained, and jury-rigged, remain the ship's most fiercely coveted amenities. Even now, impatient voices are swarming just beyond the bolted hatch in front of me--or perhaps "over" me.

The chamber is so small that from the coffin I can touch any of its six windowless walls--years in low-gravity have erased terrestrial notions such as floors or ceilings. A musk lingers from the hundreds of fevered passengers who've locked themselves in this very room for countless hours of escape. The single lamp is only bright enough to sweep the darkness into the corners and hope I won't notice. Still, the light pierces my bleary sight.

I shut my eyelids as a barricade against the invasive stimuli. But it's no use. As the torrent of breath subsides and my heartbeat retreats from my skull back into my chest, "the Hum" re-emerges, like the sand beneath the tide. The Hum--that invisible and ubiquitous white noise, somehow simultaneously heard and felt; that unnatural sonic alloy of the whir of artificial daylight, the drone of drip-fed heat and oxygen, and the rattle of myriad bolts which prevent the *Venture* from bursting apart like a pinata and releasing its 214,000 captives into the insatiable void; that inescapable reminder--the Hum is the reason a dozen day-cycles have passed since I've had a proper sleep. The reason I'm here.

And now that the rush of chimerical death has worn off, I'm eager for more. But everything--the restraints chafing my inner elbows, the sweat beads clinging like leeches to my skin, the recycled air exfoliating my nostrils, that goddamn Hum, even the Rorschach of residual light floating against the black canvas of my eyelids--everything, reminds me of the unwelcome truth: the dream has ended.

I open my eyes to check the remaining time:

00h05m12s

Dammit!

Why is waking a few minutes before an alarm so infuriating? What is a minute anyhow? Merely a subdivided duration of the orbit of a planet so distant the *Venture* won't make port there again in this lifetime. Yet our perception of time remains dictated by these vestigial metrics because it's all we bothered to teach our self-reflexive machines.

00h05m01s

Enough philosophizing. This session cost me a week of "breakfasts" and I intend to get my rations' worth. I can't afford an extra sedative; I'll have to find my own way back in.

I breathe in and out--slow, controlled--then let the black curtains fall.

Start at the end: My lungs are burning. There's no air. Launched out of the airlock again? No. There's a weight on my chest and something fluffy mashed against my face. My heartbeat quickens at the memory of helplessness. Not a bad way to go. Not nearly as exhilarating as being vaporized by a blaster or as liberating as falling two hundred stories, but not bad.

Never having been suffocated before, I'm skeptical of the machine's accuracy. For all its enhancing, extending, and control-granting power, memory and imagination--two sides of the same coin, really--remain its sole building blocks. But its every sensation is either a flawless synthesis of previous experiences or else possesses zero "real-world" comparisons. That's the beauty of a self-referential system--it's accurate even when it isn't. Efficient too. The sci-fi tales of our grandparents foretold elaborate simulators, but why waste rations and space on holodecks when each passenger already carries every conceivable desire inside his own subconscious.

Focus. Who was there? I recall an image of William Blake before a wall of gold bricks, clutching a white pillow and crouching like a wildcat. While searching for my gun, I find a Shakespeare mask at my feet. I try to put it back on, but my hands are zip-tied. It's the bank heist scenario, but something's off. I can't be hostage and robber.

Stop. Don't reason. When entering a dream, logic isn't a tool, but a barrier. You might as well try entering a river by scooping it into a bucket. Dreams don't have beginnings and endings, only points where you fall in or out of the current.

00h04m09s

Shit! Shouldn't have looked.

Just relax. Let it wash over you.

Blake and I are cramming our backpacks with gold bricks. A woman we forced to open the vault is following me, saying, "You don't have to do this." I can't see her face, but she's wearing this pastel yellow ascot with baby blue sparrows. From the lobby, I hear Byron shouting threats as he and Shelley tie up the hostages, while Coleridge and Wordsworth empty the registers. I only joined the Romantics for this one job. I need the score to pay for Mama's transplant. The woman with the yellow ascot glares disapprovingly. Sirens wail outside. Shots fired. Yeats, our getaway driver, has been gunned down in the streets. Blake puts his pistol to the manager's head, cursing him for pulling the alarm. He doesn't suspect it was me who tipped off the cops. The woman at my shoulder shakes her head. Gunshots in the lobby. Shelly is bleeding out in Byron's arms. "They're coming!" Yeats screams, rushing into the vault. The manager begs for mercy. Turns out, *he* was the one who let us in. The woman with the yellow ascot had been waiting for me inside, asleep on a bed of gold. Could it be...? BANG! The cops are breaking down the vault door. The woman rolls over--it is Eleanor!--and looks at me with piercing conviction. I know what I have to do. I tackle Blake. BANG! He fires, just missing the manager's face. We have each other by the throat when Yeats sneaks up behind me. BANG!

Awake.

00h03m02s

The hatch quivers as someone pounds from outside--"dream junkies." I've heard of them breaking in and unplugging dreamers mid-session, but I'm not worried. I've seen these malnourished insomniacs roaming the corridors, begging for rations like orphans or stowaways. Let the bastards try. They'll break their knuckles before they break the lock. A four-decade voyage will test any man's limits, but the blame for addiction rests none save the addict.

Still, I can't sleep through their racket. And I need to get back to Eleanor.

She shouldn't have been there. After the last time, I disabled recurrences. Technically, the dream was original, but it was basically a new variation on an old theme: I fight for her; she rescues me from moral suicide. Regardless, she found a way back to me. Now, it's my turn.

But the dream-junkies aren't letting up.

00h02m13s

Son of a bitch!

I check my rations. Maybe I can squeeze out another hour. I've missed breakfast by now. Can I risk skipping a few more meals? I don't want to wind up in sick bay again.

00h02m04s

Time to decide: Eleanor or reality.

I know the difference--I'm not some junkie. I know exactly how many days have passed since I abandoned her on Earth. At this point, I've spent more time with the dream than I ever did with the girl. Still, maybe we're connected somehow. Maybe she's reaching out to me across the cosmos. Or it could just be some unresolved shit my subconscious needs to work out.

Either way.

I adjust the settings:

    ROMANCE: 10

    REALISM: 8

    ABSTRACTION: 2

    VOLITION: 9

    MORTALITY: OFF.

Then, I concentrate on building an opening scene: I'm suffocating again, but this time, the pillow withdraws to reveal Eleanor, straddling me, my hands zip-tied to her golden bedposts, her wild hair half-covering a voracious smile, still wearing that yellow ascot, and nothing else.

00h01m02s

I add an hour, plus several seconds for the sedative to kick in, then transfer the rations.

01h01m11s

The light fades. The curtains fall. The clatter of the dream-junkies floats away like a kite without a string, disappears into the Hum, then both melt into the gurgle of a gentle stream. I sink into the coffin and slip down sleep's sublime current toward distant ocean dreams.

The Bleak

by Geoff Wallace

A husband and wife lived in a house infected with a machine virus. The virus made inorganic matter reconstruct itself—every time it removed one part of the house, it added an element elsewhere. Nothing was lost—just rearranged.

The house was perfectly livable; the couple simply switched rooms every few weeks. And the virus did seem to possess a sense of aesthetics. Even when it broke down a wall, the result was geometric, jagged, pleasing. The weather was astonishing. Wispy yet vivid skies, always cool yet not cold. Exceedingly pleasant. And in the backyard, a sacred tree.

The tree held balance over the region. While it lived, base impulses were kept at bay. Crime was only committed out of utmost necessity—stealing to stave off hunger, running red lights to reach the hospital in time. Darker, deeper machinations were unknown.

But then, one night, one of house's rooms suddenly appeared on the tree. There was the living room floor, a green velvet couch, and the off-white walls, all perched on a thick branch. The virus had never done that—it had always kept the couple's things in place while it transformed the house.

As the husband and wife watched, the tree began to mutate, breaking itself and sprouting new growth, flowing like a river of splintered wood. The virus had transferred itself to organic matter. The husband and wife thought maybe if they slept on the tree—a small sacrifice done slowly to appease forces unseen—the balance could be maintained. But it wasn't.

Night lasted for days; the weather turned bitter cold. The couple knew the sky was gone, never to return. As the years passed, the region collapsed. Plant life died off; animals became scarce. Architecture stagnated into stiff, unrecognizable shapes. Organized crime ruled the land, and the price was steep.

The heads of the leading crime organization resided in an enormous white-stone mansion with soaring, severe windows. A gothic mood blanketed everything. Inside, all the gangsters were dying. The virus had spread to living beings, infecting organic matter with the same disruptive, deconstructive force. A hand or foot would fall off and a new arm would sprout from elsewhere, but mangled and useless. The gangsters took it as a divine sign.

A young Dustin Hoffman, the boss's son, was writing his will beneath the dining room's once-celestial chandelier. Outwardly he only displayed a few rancid boils, but his internal organs were nearly destroyed, displaced and fused.

In the bathroom, the boss, Robert Duvall, decided his fate. He gazed out from an enormous knife-like window at the remains of the city, smoldering and distorted. The virus had replaced his skin with extraneous, partially closed blood vessels—his body oozed a viscous mixture of sweat and blood. Both his feet had dropped off, and one eye was gone entirely while another hung loose from its socket.

Everything was crumbling, decaying. The virus had even made plumbing impossible. But because the rich still had their pride, the gangsters hadn't built makeshift outhouses like most people in the region did but instead converted their bathrooms into enormous pits of porcelain.

Duvall eyed a hole in the center of the floor, thinking grimly of all the human waste inside it. Less a hole than an exit—less an exit than an abyss. He scrawled his own last words on a ragged sheet of paper. Would the virus leave it intact? He couldn't know.

The blood seeping from his broken skin gathered on the pen, trying to scab, forming a partial lasso-like blood clot around the pen.

"I only know half the hells I've set loose on this land," he wrote, laboring the pen between his liquid fingers, "but the totality of their carnage is a price I must pay alone. And I will see to it that I pay more than my own life can bear."

Somewhere in the hall, Hoffman screamed like an animal, or an animal imitating man, and Duvall paused, wondering if the virus had suddenly manifested syphilis in his son's brain. The screams filled with blood, gurgling like a blender thrown in a bathtub, and finally ceased.

Duvall grimaced and picked up the pen again. His one working eye slid further from the socket, and he cocked his head back at a grotesque angle to see the paper. He thought briefly about maneuvering it with the three working fingers on his opposite hand, but the idea made him gag.

He regained his composure and continued writing: "I have decided to send myself where I belong—in the filth. I will starve myself until I am small enough to fit inside the pit toilet, and that is where, with any luck left to me, I will drown."

He paused for a moment, thinking of what remained of his son.

"If any power still looms above…and if it retains any ounce of mercy…then I will go quickly."

Though time crawled ahead, and dehydration threatened to end him, after a small eternity the boss still stood, now a husk of a man. Both eyes gone, he groped at his skin, feeling bones sharper than before, ready to split and pierce the surface. He hadn't lost enough weight, but even with only himself as audience, he was committed to his punishment.

Summoning his final shred of strength, he grabbed his arm and pulled hard—a sickening crack shot across the tainted porcelain. Pain racked his limbs, but even pain felt good when it was delivered by his own hand; the virus couldn't touch him now.

His shoulder dislocated and body finally narrowed enough at last, he inched toward the edge of the pit and began to slide down—down into the feces and piss and blood and darkness—to drown.

Lucy

by Elizabeth Neal

Lucy wasn't certain why things kept working out the way they did. He supposed it came down to the fact that happy clowns were lucky clowns.

For years it had been the same old drudgery. Another day, another nightmare. Bouncing around the known universe, peeping into little boys' heads at odd hours had lost its edge long before. It lost its appeal shortly thereafter.

But he didn't know anything else. He knew he was dead. He didn't remember how it had happened. Quite frankly, he was resentful about it. And he knew what it felt like to die. He remembered the wet, thick, savory pop that would have been satisfactory had it been a zit and not his soul.

Other than that, Lucy did what seemed right, somehow natural. He knew how to soar high into the ethers. He'd spread his astral arms like Christ in the sunbeams. Then he'd dive, not swiftly, but deliciously slowly. A warm, palpable energy cushioned the Earth which felt like a vat of sweet meats without the stickiness. There was just that give to it followed by the feeling of being embraced, smothered. Then just when he could have gotten lost in the sensation, he'd plunge wetly into the brain matter of a random preschooler.

This was all behind him, of course. Still, sometimes he'd look back at what he considered his career with wonder. How had he gotten his inspiration for the nightmares he created? He supposed the ideas were residue of his ill-remembered life experiences. Once he had whispered into the psyche of a four year old, "This is the voice of God. You are one of the unredeemable and shall be punished with an eternal case of gas." The beauty of this being that it was mostly true. Of course, the child would have gas, who doesn't? But for the rest of his life, no matter how well he convinced the majority of his mind that it wasn't true, some small part of him thought that God was a clown, and he farted because he was damned.

There were bits that filtered through from life. Lucy fondly recalled a sexual preference attached to rabbits and select crustaceans. No way existed to engage in conjugal relations with a crustacean. Still, they did something for him. Slick wet meat with a heady smell that he couldn't fuck. So he ate it instead.

Now rabbits were a different matter entirely.

Lucy's present life wasn't so lonely either. Not since he'd learned the trick of navigating a child. The first few times he had felt fragmented, and the vessel unwieldy. The best he could accomplish was to roll the kid out of bed or make him wet his pants. Most nightmares had roughly the same response, so what was new? But once he'd found confidence in where he was going and his ability to withdraw when it felt right, there was no end to what he could do.

It had started with a boy named Tobey. Lucy had been curious about traveling beyond the cognitive branch of the brain. Slowly he oozed to the back of the head and felt a click when he tapped a neuron. At least, Lucy thought it was a neuron. In any case, there was definite cause and effect. So he'd slid back to the starting point and begun his descent again. This time though, he stretched every particle he believed he had to its fullest potential until he reached the back and the front of the kid's head. He heard the click again, but this time it was followed by clarity. Gone was the accustomed pinkish film. In its place was a ceiling covered in blue shadows, as Lucy blinked with wonder through the child's eyes. Looking through living eyes again caused a lump to rise in Lucy's astral throat, a tear to trickle down Tobey's pudgy cheek.

The thought occurred to him that this could be just the start. Surely, there was enough of him to fill a head. With his fingers pressing the buttons and a little discipline, how long would it be until he accomplished total possession?

Apparently, quite a while. But the substance that Lucy was now composed of had an elasticity that could be controlled and compromised. He could snap back to original form in an instant. He could also drip down the spinal column and flip the switches deftly.

Many months and several traumatic episodes went by before he reached maximum possession of a human child. Fortunately, the world seemed to have an endless supply of them. When he'd experimented with one, he never returned for more. Too suspicious. Careful clowns are long-lasting clowns. Make a parent anxious with repetitive irrational behavior and you end up in a medicated head. Heaven only knows what effect that could have on a spirit. A child on cough medicine tasted funny enough.

Not that Lucy would have traded those early experiences for anything. Traumatic, yes. Educational, certainly. He remembered fondly the boy in Hong Kong, the first time he'd gotten "caught in the act." Little Bruce had found, under his careful guidance, his parents' wedding album. They woke up, presumably from the noise, and found Little Bruce with a jar of mayonnaise, his pants down, making the pages sticky in a vicious frenzy. It's not pretty to whack off to images of one's mother. Little Bruce screamed, and Lucy let go. The child's cheeks flushed hot with Lucy's embarrassment. He'd counted on the kid getting caught in the morning. Never had it occurred to him that the lights would go on while he was servicing his needs. It was goddamned awkward. He took it personally for half a minute as he stared eye to eye with Bruce's father. Then he simply detached from the emotion, looked into Momma's face, and took up where he'd left off.

Lesson learned. Never confuse oneself with one's vehicle.

Through a series of complicated adventures, he'd learned many other valuable lessons: 1) Never go near the nerve ending unless you want to fry. 2) Ty-D-Bowl is flammable. And 3) never fuck a cat because it isn't the birthday party you think it's going to be.

The Proverbs of Lucy.

And why not?

One night as Little Singh floated in a tub of store brand lime flavored gelatin and bikini wax; Lucy thought to himself, "I am God." And then he thought, "Maybe I could be."

What better way to reincorporate himself into the world of the living than by speaking to the masses of young ones at night? So far he'd only whispered random cruelties and manipulated tiny fingers. If he applied himself to a singular theme, he could dethrone Jesus by the next generation. Why did he waste his genius on pranks, artful as they might be?

Could a vapor dream grand schemes?

Somehow the message had to sound good. A wannabe god didn't need to find himself shuffled off to the realm of the tooth fairy. Children already had a cadre of mythological creatures. One more wouldn't do him any good. The thing to capitalize on was their generous capacity for belief, while also including enough realism to make the pill easier to swallow. He considered name-dropping. "Well, Mohammed said licorice was a suppository." "Jesus and I go way back." But really, that sort of missed the whole point, didn't it? He didn't want to sound like anyone's lackey. Lucy needed to be loved for the miracle that was Lucy.

Perhaps, he thought, the mischief should cease. He should focus his efforts. But where to start? Tell them to love each other? They'd heard that. Tell them to hate? They already did. The spotty people hated the crooked people hated the smudged. The continuity was beautiful to behold.

All the evils possible in the world already existed: nuclear proliferation, festering sores, distrust, anxiety, murder, and shoplifting. How could the most powerful clown in history make the leap to non-corporeal cult leader on a global scale?

"I'll tell them to sleep. I'll make them hate the waking world. Look at the ugliness around you. You serve a lonely god, now. Sleep and commune with me."

Lucy frantically groped through the grey matter of a tiny girl in Iowa. There had to be an off switch. He could whisper to them. He had moved them, but he'd never met them. If he could block her perceptions of the world around her for long enough, she might turn inward and see him. Lucy was sure of it. He could become real to someone. He could velveteen rabbit his ass into the mass consciousness.

Something slid into place and the girl sighed. Her heart slowed; her eyes rolled back. "Hello." There before him stood Molly, a small shimmering substance in the shape of a child. She turned her glittery head toward the sound of his voice.

"I thought it was time you met me, Molly. My name is Lucy

and I am your God." He slowly approached the figure before him, careful not to alarm her.

"You have a burden to carry, Molly. You must tell others what you see tonight. You must tell them about me."

Molly cocked her head to one side, not appearing frightened, only curious. In fact, Lucy found himself soothed by her presence. Eons had passed since he'd communicated directly to another being. He wondered about his appearance for the first time in forever. Was he too gruesome? The shimmery substance that was Molly reached out to him. Lucy found himself shockingly self-conscious. He desired this tiny girl, not with the same urge that drove his craving for rabbits or lobsters, but in some way pure and entirely new. He ached for her approval as she stood there studying him, reaching for him.

He wanted to be worthy. Why, oh why, wasn't he glittery gold flecks? Why wasn't he bathed in perfect light and accompanied by cello music? Lucy wanted to cry.

Molly floated towards him with arms open wide. She engulfed him with a whispering sound, and the sensation of tiny fingers tickled his every particle. This was forgiving ecstasy. This was the kiss of the holy.

Lucy sighed and closed his eyes. That was his first mistake. His second was ignoring the distant chewing sound as some remote bodily process.

He didn't get a third.

In the end, Molly merely belched, and her heart sped back up to a normal resting pace.

As Lucy watched himself dissipate in the gases of the child's burp, he thought about infinity. "I do believe in eternal life! I do believe in myself reincarnate! I do believe I am a god!" He squeaked and popped into oblivion.

杀梦爱蒙 Dream of Love-Killing

by 没有人   *translation by Michael Feral*

处在迷宫般的中	*In the maze*
他们只是脚步声	*They are only footsteps to each other*
他们只是要脱单	*They only want to break aloneness*
在黑暗中	*Dark hallways*
许多走廊	*Like tiger-vines*
心跳心	*They hear each other's beating hearts*
樵夫球砍	*The woodcutter is cutting*
月亮给光	*The moon is coming out*
（她穿上了黑面具）	*(she puts on her black mask)*
在这儿, 说她, 打切	*Here, she says, I am Robbery-by-Cutting*
（她用刀着他的背）	*(she points her knife in his back)*
钱还是身, 他问	*My money or my body?*
给我钱, 她回答	*Your money, she says*
没有钱	*No money, he says*
给我身	*Your body, she says*
是你的	*You have it, he says*
给我心	*Take my heart, she says*
是你的	*I have it, he says*
给我月亮	*But give me the moon, she says*

（他穿上了黑色面具）　　　　　　　*(he puts on his black mask)*

我爱你，打切　　　　　　*I love you, Robbery-by-Cutting, he says*

在月亮里面，伐木工削减了 *Inside the moon, the woodcutter cuts*

The Anchor

by Kummam Al-Maadeed

It was dark and so quiet, so very quiet.

It was late at night, so it was to be expected, but as I laid on my bed with the fire all died out and the air so still around me, it felt so empty, so lonely.

The anxiousness of my heart sent an invisible rope slithering around my neck, suffocating me. The agitation took hold of my body, as if someone threw a net at me, wrapping me, sinking deep into my skin.

Minutes passed and the net felt tighter and tighter; my mind overwhelmed by the screeching screams of my soul, my lungs restless by the lack of air.

Get out, my mind shouted at me. I shot up.

My feet, touching the cold floor, moved on their own, knowing the way, as I opened door after door and ran through the mansion's corridors. I ran and I ran, my vision blurred, blind to my surroundings, the ones I got so accustomed to the past few months. I could not breathe or feel any comfort, until I shoved the glass doors wide open and ran out to the balcony and down the stairs, not caring about the stinging feeling from the freezing cold.

I halted and gasped at the sight of the wide free land before me. The lands that held no borders, no walls and no limitations. My soul burst with energy and ruptured its captive net, air shot through my lungs.

I called for more air as I stood there, shaking, not from the cold, no, I welcomed the frosting breeze that soothed my skin, no, I shook from the fear of being trapped, from being crushed by the walls I just ran from. But as I stood there with nothing around me, I let go of the fear, feeling it seep out of my skin, like water evaporating to fog.

"It's quite beautiful." I heard his voice. I turned and he stood there, behind me, keeping himself at a distance. He was wearing his riding cloths and traveling cloak. Did he just returned from his trip to town, or was he going out again?

"Why are you here?" I huffed and gazed at the scene before me again.

"Why shouldn't I?" he said, as calm as always. "You don't want me to be here?"

I always want you here, I thought, but did not say it. "I hate it when you see me like this."

"Like what?"

"Like a mad woman," I whispered.

"You don't look like a mad woman," he said, his voice sounding closer, but I didn't turn. "You look scared." He was right next to me.

"I needed to breath," I said, resisting every urge to throw myself at him.

"Then breath. As much as you like."

I looked at him. His eyes weren't joking, or judging, but told me something I longed to hear; I understand.

He ungloved his right hand and slid it around my clenched fist, reminding me to relax it. His touch was warm and I shuddered.

"Can I offer you my cloak?" he said, cautiously.

My body locked up and I pulled my hand from his. I shook my head. I couldn't bear the thought of something wrapping me.

He nodded and took his cloak off. I panicked at the possibility that he might force me to wear it.

But of course he would never do that. He spread his cloak on the ground before me and offered me his hand. I hesitated, but then took it. He pulled me to stand on the cloak and when both my feet were on it, he kneeled down and pushed the cloak around my feet, slightly covering my legs.

Holding his hands away from the cloak, he lifted his face up at me and said, "Is that all right?"

I nodded and I knew I failed in holding back a smile, as he winked at me before getting up.

As my feet all wrapped up in warmth and his presence next to me, I felt every inch of me finally relaxed.

"I hate my room." I said finally.

"Then we will change it."

"I want the one on the second floor with the balcony. The one no one uses."

He raised his eyebrows at me and laughed. It was so blunt of me to request that, but it was what I needed. I couldn't be running like this every night. Everyone living in the mansion thought I was too crazy already.

"I'm not going to throw myself out of the balcony." I blurted out when he didn't respond.

"Hey," he tugged my elbow, "I know you won't"

"Why not? It's what's everyone is going to tell you." I pulled my elbow out of his reach.

"Because," He stood before me, facing me, his face serious, "Yes, you are quite mad sometimes, but I know that you are as much sane as you are mad. I trust you."

And this time, I couldn't hold myself back and leaned on him; my head on his chest and my hands gripping his shirt.

He laughed, relieved, and wrapped my body with his arms and brought me closer.

And I felt it then, every piece of me that was shattered from that fear and suffocation found its rightful place again in my soul and I allowed his reassuring energy to strengthen my spirit.

"So, can I have that room, then?" I said and I smiled so wide, as I felt his laugh anchoring me back to myself.

Only in My Dreams
by Andy Anderson

<Excerpts from a 10-year-old dream journal>

We were in Africa.

I lived in a super fancy house.

We walked everywhere.

I was like this is impossible on a pogo stick.

I was on a long journey.

I broke my arm.

I was hanging out with hippies and the homeless.

I was cleaning bathrooms somewhere.

I was invited to go to Thailand.

I blew up Tiffs car.

I married Tinny.

I was late for school.

I needed to go to Lubbock.

I went into a club.

The system was down.

I was with my family.

I went to a movie theater but the kids showed up and we had to decide whether or not to drink the already purchased alcohol.

I paid for the movies with three dollars then used my debit card.

I brought leftover Mac & Cheese.

David suggested that if I love The Philippines so much, why don't I just move there?

"Arielle is Hamming" helped me come out to my Dad.

"Ash came home last night."

I was at a wedding.

I was at my moms house and she told me that on Tuesday I was gonna go on this date with a boy.

I was in a hostage situation.

I was leaving for a long journey but didn't want to go.

I didn't want to go.

I was running late.

Then

    I woke up for real, running late, and #confused.

Japan Dream

by Mickey Collins

I came to Japan for one reason only: to try the best sushi. Apparently a new place opened up and it was so the rage. My traveling partner was still fighting off jet lag so I set off on my own.

The place wasn't too hard to find, there was a streetcar that dropped you off right there, only I missed it the first time and as it was a one-way ride I had to ride it all the way around again. But I was determined.

There wasn't much of a line to get in. Only one guy ahead of me. I eavesdropped a bit. The guy at the window asked what he wanted. The man in line said sushi.

Window man: 2nd floor. And it'll cost you to check your coat in.

Man in line: no it won't. It didn't last time I was here. I'm leaving my coat on.

The window man grumbled but allowed entrance to the man.

I was next. I took off my coat. I was prepared to do anything to eat the sushi.

What're you here for? The window man asked me.

2nd floor, sushi I said. And here's my coat. I was ready.

The man smiled and allowed me in.

Inside was much busier. The second floor sushi restaurant seemed more like a bar. It was cramped, it was dark. One side had a counter where people were lined up. There were small circular tables throughout the room where people stood and ate and talked. One corner had a jukebox that played some incomprehensible loud music.

I got in line, trying to make out what the sign said. Under inari there were four options, none of which sounded familiar. This had to be the best sushi place.

Someone behind me was saying I cut in line. I turned and there was an angry group of people crowded up. I bowed and went behind them. Then I saw another line next to ours that was much shorter. I line jumped, causing another uproar from the group. But I didn't care.

I don't remember ordering but soon enough I was at a table with my plate of inari. It looked familiar enough, the simple soybean skins like tents over the sushi rice safe inside and a sprinkling of sesame seeds on top. There was also a side of beans and seaweed salad.

I picked up a red bean between my chopsticks and thought of my friend, who had traveled all this way with me, only to be stuck in the hotel. I could picture what he was doing so vividly and as I focused on him that before I knew it I was him. We (he and I) were in the hotel room where I left him. We were in bed. I felt sad. Sad because I was alone. Sad because the reason behind this whole trip was that his father had just passed and left him with some money. The only thing he wanted to do was take a trip to Japan. He invited me along since we were friends and I could help him get out of his funk. And then I had gone and left him alone to fulfill my selfish dream.

He was sleeping in the hotel, cursed by jet lag, while I had pushed through and ran off. His dreams were of his dad, and of home, and of me. He dreamed of the day his father got married. They were in a church, my friend was the ring bearer, and everything seemed happy. And then the dream morphed. As my friend walked down the aisle, the church transformed into a movie theater. Now he was in a seat watching a movie, while his church shoes got stuck to the floor. The movie was an old Western, I think. And my friend sat there in the theater alone eating popcorn. As he chewed I chewed. And I felt sad again.

Then I was back to myself, in the sushi restaurant. The bean had left my chopsticks' grip and that's what I was chewing on. I swallowed. A tear flowed down my cheek.

It was just so tasty.

The Sea of Transformation

by Geoff Wallace

The house was expensive, endless, and normally boring. Cheap 1990s fake-hardwood lofts, fake antique ceiling fans. But it was the time of the great competition, and every room was full with NBA stars. Shaq was downstairs, sprawled out on a sectional, but it was a discount Shaq—the Shaq from *Minecraft*.

The house thrummed with activity; I needed air. I went outside to the white-sand beach and sunny ocean beyond. As I walked to the shoreline, the small furry creature on my shoulder grew uneasy.

"Are we in Thailand?" I asked, gazing out at the lush columnar islets littering the waters. "I feel like I've seen these tiny islands in a movie—"

"No!" it said, its too-large eyes flashing neon. "This is the Sea of Transformation. You must be careful!"

I looked back at the house—something was happening on the teak porch, limbs were waving and a barking swarmed around them, but I couldn't tell what it was, so I turned back to the sea. *The outside of the house is teak*, I thought, *but everything inside is laminate.* I waded into the sea until the water reached my chest, my lungs beginning to constrict.

"This is the point of no return," the small furry creature said. "You must be mindful!"

I narrowed my eyes and became calm. As the waves curled toward me, every tiny edge of crust, every last water molecule, transformed. Foam became fish, the froth blossomed into anemones, sea cucumbers, jellyfish, green-blue shallows boiled up into blinding, violent light. What was once water writhed around me, its tidal movement now the groans of a vast singular organism.

"No!" I shouted. "No, no, no!"—and spontaneously found myself back on the porch, running into the house yelling "Murder! There's been a murderrr!" But as I spoke the last word, my mouth slurred, and everything became hilarious, like it was a game. "Let's find that dog!" I yelled. "The one that was barking!"

Kids spilled out of the rooms, ready to play. Nobody asked me about the murder, they only cared about the game, but I knew Shaq could help. He was now in the biggest living room, lounging in front of a 1990s-style laminate wood entertainment center, watching TV as he waited for the tournament to start.

Something was off about Shaq. His jersey was wrong, all steel gray, and the cold colors made him seem detached, adrift. Sensing my gaze, he laughed quietly. "You should try the front porch," he said, his mood so somber the air around him felt weighted. He laughed again, sending a shiver zagging across my shoulders, and I hurried out to the front porch. I glanced around wildly—too wildly—and fell on my back. Looking up, I saw five glowing spheres hovering in geometric formation above me, just beneath the porch roof.

"Where's the dog?" I asked. "And is he with Death? Or is the dog Death?"

"We are the ones transformed," the spheres said. "But the dog—and Death—"

A vision of an enormous smile appeared in my head.

"Wait!" I begged. "I know who you were!"

But they flew away.

Short Story

by Alexander Demitrus

He always wrote about his bittersweet nightmares. They always consisted of her; Ryan Durst never remembered anything else really. She would come to him and look as beautiful as ever. They would hold hands and walk around the lake, noticing the changing colors of the scenery; she would apologize for leaving over and over again. He would, every single time, forgiver her and pine for her attention in any way possible.

But last night's was different. She had one last thing for him to do before they could be together. She wanted him to follow her to take a swim together in the lake, just as they had on their first date when they fell in love. Ryan obeyed; he wanted her so badly it hurt. As he held her by the hips in the shallow water, she turned on him and pushed him playfully into the water. He tried to get up but couldn't. He woke up in a shivering sweat. He hated how he remembered that part.

The air was freezing. It hadn't been this cold in a long time. In all his years, Ryan had never shivered on his morning walk. The dew had frozen on the grass, creating a fake white tipped landscape that would melt as soon as the sun's rays decided to poke through the clouds.

It was mornings like these that Ryan missed her. The cold wind that gently brushed his face reminded him of her soft hands. It was those hands that would hold his face in front of hers so that they could stare into each other's eyes.

"How long will you love me for, Ryan?"

"Forever" he would reply. And he meant it too. He had loved her for so long and never planned to stop. He could remember her eyes exactly to this day. Her hazel shaped green eyes reminded Ryan of emeralds that sparkled under a gem cutter's light. Even though she would constantly complain for attention and say, "They're just as green as anyone else's", he would disagree.

"They're the most beautiful green I have ever seen," Ryan would say. Her round cheeks would blush to a deep, full red and she would look at the ground, hiding her pink lips from him. It was like clockwork, her personality. He would compliment her and she would turn away, knowing how beautiful she really was, yet trying to be modest and coy.

The sun was just started to melt the dew. As he walked along shivering, he remembered how the sunlight had hit her black hair. The thick waves had bounced beams of light wherever she walked and constantly caught attention. Her milky skin refracted sunlight to show her skinny torso that led down to beautiful full legs attached to feet that were always in high heels. He knew she made heads turn whenever she was out somewhere, but she wanted nothing to do with anyone else. He was lucky; she had only ever loved him.

"Where will we live and grow old together, Ryan?"

"Where do you want to be?" he would reply. And with that response she would talk about all the adventures they would have together. They would hike mountains and travel the world and swim in every ocean this planet had to offer. They could try every type of food together and eventually settle down in their home town. They would have one child, a boy, which would have her eyes and personality.

The clouds overhead that morning were an abysmal gray. Ryan wished that it wasn't so dark outside. Though it was winter, the landscape had yet to been caked with a white snow. Instead, the trees remained dead, uncovered, their branches reaching up towards the sky with no leaves grasping towards the heavens praying for warmer weather. It had been a long time, too long, since he had done this walk with her really there.

He passed the grassy hill where they would lay down together and watch the clouds form shapes overhead. They would hold hands and joke and laugh about all the silly things the clouds formed in the sky. They would talk about their future and everything that life held for them. "The world is our oyster, Ryan;, there is nothing holding us back. We'll be in love forever. Forever and ever and ever and ever…" Her voice would fade out as he became lost in her eyes.

"What are you looking at?" she would question him.

"Oh," he would say being brought back to reality, "just you."

Ryan continued walking on, alone, wondering what should have been. He looked up at the clouds which had melded together to create a barrier between him and the heavens. No shapes could be formed out of the gray blobs that trekked across the melancholy sky. He dropped his gaze back to the ground. The leaves blew past him like tumbleweeds as the wind picked up. He grabbed his coat and wrapped it tighter around his body. He decided to head home.

He walked up to the door of his house and fumbled around with his keys. Suddenly, he heard a voice, a woman's voice in his home. He was confused. No one had been here since she had left. He found his correct key and burst through the door and gazed down the hallway. He saw her, he was sure of it, running toward down the hallway toward the bedroom. His heart jumped. It had been years since he had seen her. He could smell her favorite perfume, hint of lilac, as he started toward the bedroom. He got to the corner of the hallway and turned to see the door closing and heard a giggle. He could still smell her. The perfume was stronger with every step toward the bedroom door. He put his hand on the doorknob which was icy to the touch. Shivers went up his spine and he stopped in his tracks. He was shivering again, as if the wind from outside had followed him in.

"Ryan, baby, come inside. I've missed you," he heard on the other side of the door.

His mind was racing. He knew it couldn't be real, yet he wanted to believe it was true. He opened the door. She was there, wearing his favorite black cocktail dress, sitting in the chair in the corner of the room. Ryan stumbled over to her and dropped to his knees incredulously. She was so beautiful. Her skin was fair and her body hadn't changed at all. Every feature was as perfect as he remembered. Her lips were pink and full and her eyes were as deep a green as emeralds. He picked up her hand in hers. It was warm to the touch. She smiled at him and caressed his face.

"Ryan, I'm home. I told you I would be back."

"How is this possible?" Ryan exclaimed. "You left...?" He was unsure of himself. What had really happened? Where had she been? How was she here right now?

"Sweetie, it's alright. I'm here now, that's all that matters."

Ryan put his head on her lap. She warmed his entire body and continued to caress his head. "Don't leave me again. Please, don't ever leave me again," he said as the tears welled up in his eyes. He looked up at her and knew this was for real. He knew he was right all along. Everyone told him she would never come back; and now they were all proved wrong. The tears stung the corners of his eyes as they began to fall down his cheeks. She tried to wipe them away, but they kept falling down. Ryan Durst let himself melt into her and allowed tear after tear to fall into her lap as she held him with a reassuring and warming grip.

"Baby, let's go for a walk together. Just you and me, like old times," she said after he had finished.

He immediately sprang to his feet and grabbed her heavy coat. "I'll be fine dear," she said as she started to walk toward the front of the house, sashaying her dress while she left the room. Ryan threw on his thick jacket and bounded after her, opening the door as he always did and followed her into the blistering cold.

They held hands. Her hands were so warm that his entire body seemed affected by the heat she was giving off. Ryan assumed it was due to his extreme elation that made his blood pump furiously. She led the way down to their usual path, the one he had completed a round on nearly ten minutes ago. They went an unusual way, winding around the river going counter clockwise instead of their regular direction. Ryan assumed it was because she wanted to get to the tree where they had marked their initials on that was by the water. He was right.

They stopped right by the giant oak tree that held two initials within a heart. They read:

R.D. + L.S.

"Remember when we carved these, baby? It was the first time you told me you loved me. The first time you told me you would love me forever."

Ryan remembered that day. She had been as perfect as she was now. Not a single thing had changed about her. He combed his hand through his hair and pushed her face towards his. He was lost in her eyes yet again. He fell into them and continued to fall into an eternal green abyss that reflected light and love all around him. It wasn't until she pulled away that his falling sensation proceeded to stop in his stomach.

She got up and stroked the indents of the initials in the tree. Ryan followed her and stood behind her, his hands around her hips with his head on her shoulder beside her head. She giggled, knowing all she had to do was get up for him to follow

"Don't ever leave me again," he said in a serious tone. He flipped her around so she was facing him. "I mean it, baby. I can't hold myself together when you aren't around. I love you so much. I always will."

"I know you do. I know you will," she said softly as her hand reached up to caress his face. "But I needed time, to know that you were true to me. I wanted to make sure you could surpass any test for me. And now there's only one more. One more until we can be together."

"Of course, let me know what it is baby, I can do it this minute. Don't hold out on me for anything longer. It's already been ten years." Ryan nodded as he spoke to her. He was so excited; he wouldn't have to wait any longer as of today.

"I want you to tell me you love me how you did the first time. Let's fall back in love like we did before," she said.

"Alright baby." Ryan's mind was moving at a mile a minute. "I can do that. I'll do it for you." The thought of holding onto her forever was the only thing on his mind. He started to undress down to his briefs while she walked to the edge of the water. When he was ready, he met her down at the water's edge and they waded in together, hand in hand.

The frigid water felt like knives piercing his skin and digging into his bones. Every part of his body screamed as he slowly stepped farther and farther into water. The warmth from her hands had subsided, leaving him completely vulnerable to the freezing lake. She let go of his hand and dipped her body completely in and shot up from the water, her hair glistening in the winter sun. Ryan dropped to her knees. He shivered while he worked up the courage to dump himself backwards into

the frigidness that surrounded him. He plunged the back of
his head into the water. His heart pounded and screamed. He
came up gasping, but, before he could catch his breath, he was
forced under by his neck with a tight locked grip. He stared up
at her, her beautiful black hair shimmering and her emerald
green eyes pierced his gaze. His lungs grappled for fresh oxygen
as he tapped her arm; yet she stared down at him, not breaking
her stare. Ryan had confidence she would let him up until her
grip increased in strength. He yelled underwater frantically,
but only a gurgling and surge of bubbles was released. He could
see her mouthing "I'm sorry" as *her* voice in the back of his
head said, "It will all be over soon Ryan, it will all be over soon."
Ryan's vision started to get hazy as his arms fought to release
her grip which wouldn't let up an inch. He felt himself getting
weaker, as the pangs of pain in his lungs increased, deprived of
what they craved. *Her* voice kept repeating the same words, "It
will all be over soon Ryan, it will all be over soon," as he felt his
arms drop back into the frigid waters of the lake. With his last
ounce of strength, he gurgled into the water, "I love you," and
then felt nothing.

Wrinkles and Calluses

by Z.B. Wagman

The only thing I remember about my nana is her hands. They were not the soft, Toll House baking hands of America's favorite grandma. They were hard. Hard and wrinkled and full of calluses. They were the hands of a woman who spent far too many years out in the fields, toiling under the sun to put food on our table.

When I was younger, I used to dream about those hands—nightmares really. The way they would come down tougher than boards when I was bad. "Anyone but nana," I used to cry as she would haul me across her lap. I get phantom pains just thinking about those spankings.

And then one day they weren't there any more. Those hands that spoke of hardwork and hard times were gone. There was no relief in my mind, no remembrance of those old spankings. Instead, it was as if an immutable force had disappeared over night, as if gravity had stopped working and I was left floating all alone amongst the stars.

I barely remember the funeral. There were lots of people I did not recognize and very few I did. People told stories of my nana—a person who was quick to joke and quicker to laugh, a person who always tried to help no matter the burden. They told stories of someone so different from the person whom those hands belonged to that I started to wonder if I was in the wrong place. Had I wandered into a different funeral? A funeral for a different nana who probably baked her grandkids the softest chocolate chip cookies?

By the time it was my turn in front of the casket I was convinced that my nana would not be the one lying there. Some other old lady would be enshrined in flowers. It had been her doting family who had been apologizing for my loss. I waddled up to the casket so sure in my mistake that I did not recognize the woman lying there. She was not wrinkled enough to be my nana. Nor did she have the perpetual scowl my nana always wore. And then I saw her hands.

They were yellow and stiff, so unnatural that I thought they were fake. But I recognized the way they clutched at each other, as if the world had spent decades trying to tear them apart. They looked harder now, less like boards and more like pieces of granite. She would like that, knowing how much harder she could whoop me. And I recognized the callouses; the blood and sweat that had gone into making those hands hard. They were the hands of a fighter, the hands of someone who struggled all her life trying to do the right thing. They were the hands of my nana.

A Quick Personal Tour of My Dreams

by Dan Heise

When I was young, I dreamed of being a baseball player.

A common Midwest dream

I played second base in Little League

Smoothed the dirt in front of me, waited for my opportunity.

A good glove, an awful bat though.

I struck out more times than I can count,

Realized this wasn't a living

This was just a hobby I enjoyed doing.

In eighth grade I wrote a newspaper article for an assignment

My teacher loved it

She told me I could be a journalist

Suddenly my future started to open up in front of me

I wrote short stories and poems

People asked what I wanted to do for college

And for the first time I had an answer

"I want to be journalist," I would say

Writing didn't seem so farfetched any more

I began to look at journalism schools

Mizzou seemed like a good choice, I could live with my grand-mother in Columbia.

That is, until my junior year

When by chance I was watching Fight Club (with commentary)

And I realized how fun it would be to be an actor

I told my parents I wanted to study theater

They were immediately on board and helped me look for schools

My dream becoming a reality

Then came the applying, auditioning, waiting

Acceptance, rejection, decision.

I chose a school. I followed my dream.

I graduated. I am still following my dream.

Those are the capital D Dreams I have had;

The ones people always wanna know about.

The ones they ask about.

"What did you wanna be when you grow up?

What did you dream of doing?"

They never wanna know about the smaller ones.

They never wanna know about my sophomore year of high school

When I formed a band that practiced once

Dreaming of becoming rock stars, like half my high school.

We played through Steady As She Goes by the Raconteurs in
my basement

And that was the end of that.

They never wanna know about the time I cut off a sliver of my
left middle finger

While chopping basil at a job I hated

And immediately dreamed of telling this story on a talk show as
a famous actor.

They never wanna know about turning 24 and wanting to move
to Portland

Because Portland had more television show opportunities than
St. Louis

And I dreamed of one day being in television.

I achieved that dream,

After standing behind the scenes of "The Librarians" for 10
hours,

In the most uncomfortable shoes ever,

And yet I still had the biggest grin on my face.

But they never wanna know about after that.

How I cried to my parents less than a month later

Because I hated my roommate and I couldn't find any other
work.

I dreamed of something terrible happening so I would have an
excuse to move back home.

They never wanna know about senior year of college

When I wrote the first poem I actually loved

("Does It Mean Anything When a Girl Wears My Shorts")

And thought that maybe I was ok at this whole writing thing

And dreamed of showing everyone.

They never ask about later my senior year

When I finished writing my first play

("Janus (Like the God)")

And gained even more confidence in this whole writing thing

And dreamed of everyone seeing it.

They never wanna know about how I finished my second play recently

("I Will Betray You, and I Will Kill You")

And I have still submitted nothing

Yet I still dream of my works being read and performed.

They never wanna know about turning thirteen and falling in love on the internet with a girl in Montana

And how I fell so head over heels in love with her I dreamed of being with her forever.

They never wanna know about how she got married 8 years later

And now every once in a while I dream of her at night and feel guilty, yet I still miss her.

They never wanna know about how sometimes, I dream of her coming to Portland

So I can finally say hello in person.

They never wanna know about how I still sometimes dream of

something terrible at home happening

Just so I have an excuse to go back

Because some days I get so homesick I can't stand it.

They never wanna know about my daydreams,

And how half of them involve people saying good things about me when I'm not around.

No one asks about the lowercase D dreams I have had.

The dreams scattered in between all the other ones

And no one ever

Ever

EVER

Asks me about my DREAM

All capital letters.

The large one that prevails over everything else I do.

The one I discovered my senior year of high school.

I want to inspire.

I want to make people happy

I want to be kind, so others will be kind.

I want to help, so others will help.

I want to be myself, so others will know that they can be themselves.

In the end,

I will inspire you.

And you cannot stop me from dreaming this.

 I dream.

I Dream.

I DREAM.

Skin

by Carole Reichstein

Marty's maternal family came from the Creek Indian tribe of Alabama. His grandfather, who went by Buck, talked like Foghorn Leghorn and was full blood Creek Indian. When Marty was a boy, he went fishing with Buck. Marty stood up to grab the bait box and fell into the river. He couldn't swim, so he flailed, gasped, and began to sink to the bottom. Buck grabbed Marty's t-shirt and hauled him back into the boat. NOW QUIT YOUR FOOLING AROUND he yelled as Marty sucked in air. Buck lived to be 100 years old. He died in his John Deere tractor while plowing a field.

Marty never really talked about his tiny bit of Native American blood inside him. He wore his hair long, but only so he could sweep it back dramatically with his big hands while he told a funny story. He looked more like a member of a Viking heavy metal band than anything else. Still, sometimes a man would pass Marty on the street and see the pale brown birthmark near his temple. It was shaped like a tiny kidney. Marty said that was a common birthmark for someone who is part white and part Native American. Sometimes Indians passed him on the street and gave him a once-over, nodded, and said "Skin." Marty explained that meant hey dude you are kind of related to me and that's cool.

Marty ate lots of Tums and Alka Seltzer. He'd been overweight for years and his stomach pains were a normal routine. We even had Alka Seltzer tablets decorating our tables at our wedding (Marty chose the wedding decorations, décor and flowers). He assumed that he just had acid reflux and also drank lots of milk of magnesia. His looks changed slowly over time. Meanwhile, our daughter was born in 2007, and he got a new job working at a computer sales gig at 6am. We slept in separate bedrooms so Marty could get enough sleep for his earlybird job, and I could nurse Claire throughout the night without waking up Marty. He worked 6am to 3pm, and I worked 1-9pm. Three years blurred by, full of love, but also fraught with financial stress, family drama and fatigue. In December 2009, I got Marty on my health insurance. Marty was almost 45 but looked much older. I wanted him to get his teeth cleaned and maybe the doctor would encourage him to lose weight and cut down on his smoking and curb his bad Pabst habit.

On January 30th, 2010, Marty made me drive him to the ER for his severe stomach pain. I packed Claire into the car and we all went together. Hours went by, and finally, a doctor thought to give Marty an MRI. Stage 4 colon cancer was the root of his pain. The doctors guessed that this hard mass in his stomach had incubated in there for years.

Marty was an unreliable narrator. He fudged facts and sometimes did things he shouldn't have. I don't know how much time he was given to live by his doctor. Marty said that he had maybe 5 years, but when his 46th birthday came 9 months later, he threw himself a GIANT birthday party and the theme was "beating the odds." So obviously the doctor didn't expect him to even make it that long. Every person on the west coast who knew Marty showed up at our house. Our daughter Claire stayed up until 2am with a sweet child attending the party with her parents. I put Claire to bed. She had a blast. The next morning, she woke up, looked around, and said, Where did all the people go?

Two years of chemotherapy treatments, hospitals, medical trials and colostomy bags went by. I put on a brave face and concentrated on working my 40 hours a week and NOT GETTING FIRED from my job so Marty would continue to have the best medical care possible. Denial is an extremely helpful tool in this situation. The only way out is through, we told each other. As long as Marty was alive in this moment, that was all that mattered. We took bike rides, celebrated Claire's next 2 birthdays, and hung on tight. And we continued on this path until March 2012, when Marty's body just said, I can't fucking fight this anymore.

The phone rang at 3am. I woke cleanly from my jumbled dream and answered it. This is the doctor on call at St Vincent. Marty has taken a turn for the worse and you need to get over here, he said.

Can I go back to sleep? I said. I'm tired and I just fell asleep about an hour ago.

No, you need to be here right now.

I called my friend Mary, a union organizer. I wish that everyone who ever finds themselves in this terrible situation could have a union organizer friend to help them through the shit. She picked me up in the middle of the night, and Karen and Denis came over to take Claire. We got to Marty's bedside at 5am. It was still dark. He was on his way. An incubator helped him breathe in a jerky, labored way. I knew Marty was really dying then, because I had seen my father breathe the same way as he died 3 years before.

While we kept vigil at his bedside, my mother and my stepfather were 30,000 feet in the air, flying from Florida to Portland to try and make it in time to say goodbye to Marty. The room felt electric and static-y like a vacuum tube, like there wasn't anything else in the world except his hospital room and the hospital that contained it. Nick. Karen. Denis. Sarah. Jesse. Annie. Nena. Mary. Tommi. There were more people but my memory from that day and night is like a blurry and fraught gauze.

The last time I was in a hospital room for that long was when I gave birth to our child. The world had ended and fallen away. All that was left were my doctor, the wonderful nurses, and Marty, who held my hand and gave me ice chips while I pushed for 4 hours. I thought we would never leave that womb of a room.

Now we were in a different room. The nurses gave Claire paper and crayons and toys while Marty did his death work. We labored with him. Claire said to no one in particular, "Instead of a birthday, today is my Daddy's dying day!" A nurse widened her eyes and mouthed "OH MY GOD" to us.

Marty died at 10:47pm. It was a Thursday.

Mom and Harry arrived about an hour later.

Claire ran into her grandmother's arms and my Mom said I'm here for you, grandma is here. My mother turned to me. "What time did he pass away?"

"10:47," I said. "About an hour ago."

"Marty appeared to me in a dream while I was in the airplane," she said. "Marty was singing a Native American death song and he wanted me to join in." But I don't know the words, my Mom said. Yes you do, Susie, said Marty, you've always known the words. And they began to chant together. The dream was so real and vivid that when she woke, she asked my step-dad what time it was. "It's 10:47," Harry said.

The last time I saw Marty in a dream, his hair was short and he wore those black glasses that I still have in a closet some-where. He was turned away from me, standing, reading a book in some godhead bookstore of some sort. I ran to say HI! HI! HI! to him, but before I could get there I woke up. As I always do.

Lullaby

by Ben Talley

Watch her now as she performs the ritual. She is not who you think she is. Yes, she may still be the librarian who smiles as you go in for your study sessions on weeknights. Or she may be that front-of-house friend you had keeping you sane as you worked the morning shifts together a couple jobs ago, whom you haven't spoken to since quitting. Or she may even be the aunt on your stepfather's side who seems nice, but keeps to herself and you keep to yours and that's all very fine. But then there is the ritual, an evening act no one has witnessed in all her unknown years here until now. She shows you, has invited you to her home this particular day because by the laws of this plane her time is running short. She has aged; the ritual can only be performed by her so many more times before she succumbs to the earth, as we all do. And for whatever reason, of everyone she has met in this world you are chosen, you are her most trusted to see the ritual continued.

Watch carefully. Take note.

Listen.

She closes the door behind you. Standing at her heels you absorb the room. It is quaint, somehow just as you imagined it to be. Maroon drapes shutter the windows, furniture sparsed about, a chest high dresser to the left, a full body mirror to the right of it. The centerpiece: a king sized bed, commanding the space as such, leaving little room for legs to circle around it.

Without looking back at you she disrobes. Were it not for the prior discussion between you about the events to transpire you would be taken aback at her candor. As she approaches the bed, however, you realize that she has absented you from her focus. She has succumbed to the ritual.

Looming beside the bed she peels back the duvet and top sheet in one, revealing a door. It is a simple, single wooden door, windowless, not unlike what would be found as the entrance to any common neighborhood home. It lies there, not on top of the mattress, but sunken in lightly, to be level with the top of the cushion.

She climbs into bed with the natural non-grace of any normal human, though at this point it has become clear to you that that is a naïve observation. Otherworldly events transpire here.

Pulling the covers over her body the woman nuzzles into a comfort. Her body rests atop the door, nestled carefully within its frame. She closes her eyes. You stand there immovable, afraid of the slightest creak from your shifting body interrupting her drift.

It is but moments before she is asleep.

With the fading of her consciousness the door slowly opens beneath her. Now you approach, to keep her in view.

Down she floats on lunar-like gravity, sinking deep and deeper into a dark cerulean void. Her hair spreads out with the porosity of water as she falls. Past her body you see the truth.

Mountainous from head to toe, curled up like a fetus in womb, is the colossal god, or God if the spirit allows. You, a dream, can see the Dreamer. The One for whom the reality you live in, universe and all, is nothing more than an unconscious fantasy. The One whom in the threat of waking, can blink you and everything you know out of existence.

Listen closely, for here is the remedy to that nightmare for which we all fear.

She sings to It.

A gentle, harmonious, soporific lullaby. A spell of her own making to keep God under. The same song she used in the Beginning to put It to sleep in order to escape a judgment for unknowable crimes in the realm she fled from.

Successfully she has hidden here, the real world to us and a dream refuge to her. Living an honest life to repay her sins in another, performing the ritual each night till her last. The lullaby that must never not be sung to the dreaming.

Soon she will be able to sing it no more.

Listen closely.

Wrong Elevator

by L. Fid

The entrance to the conveyance is getting smaller; the rectangle closing towards a vertical slit.

Our arrival, however, pauses the doors -- just enough. We turn sideways and squeeze through.

We're in. The doors whoosh shut. Ding.

We're moving before we realize we're on the wrong elevator.

Too late.

We drop towards terminal velocity and float towards the ceiling. Soon after freefall, our box swings to the left and then back up, in a giant arc. We re-enter another shaft and start accelerating upwards, then jerk to the side, back up, and then to the side for a good long time.

As the thrust lessens, we can lift our arms from the wall. One of us, another passenger, reaches

with some effort and presses a floor button.

We fall, fall.

And fall.

When it seems that we -- all of us (as we've all made eye contact by now, the travelers, and the soul count is complete) -- intuit that the bottom of the gravity well, our astonishingly violent demise, lay just moments away... We're pulled into a different trajectory, another arc, but violently manipulated this time, as if by a giant hand. Terrifyingly random jerks toss us this way and that.

Wham, clunk! Now we're heading downward, headfirst. We've entered another structure.

Our box rattles into place and starts to move at something closer to normal speed. We crumple into the carpet, our bodies shocked at the sudden return of normal gravity. The disentanglement is awkward and long.

Not everyone has survived.

Ding. The doors whoosh open.

One of the passengers crawls onto the metal seam and collapses, heaving and weeping. Another limps past, then staggers away.

We gather ourselves up as best we can, supporting a tentative ascent with hands, shoulders, and walls. You stoop back down to help the injured. We haul them out, one by one -- alive, dead, and everyway between.

At last we come to the first, the body lying across the doorway, quietly whimpering, staring past the carnage into the curving marble hall. You have the arms, I have the legs, but when we lift, the person lets out a gasp and we fall.

It's just me now, and the person's lower half -- one-and-a-half passengers -- in free fall once more. You, back with the bodies and your own burden of guts and woe, gone forever. Me, floating inside a bloody soup can in the wind.

I reach through the goo and entrails, press every button.

We jerk left right, down and up. Again and again.

I let myself go flaccid, hope for a quick, merciful snap of the neck.

Ding.

I crawl out into a bright alien world. Giant monsters hover over me, cooing.

All you do in Hell is...

by Geoff Wallace

I attended a paint party at an aunt's house with my boyfriend Stephen. Everyone was following the newest fashion: leave everything in the house where it is and cover it in paint. We watched in awe as they dumped bright green paint over a pile of magazines on the kitchen counter.

I left and caught a plane to Minnesota—all the seats faced rearwards. I landed in SF instead and met my stepbrother, Eldon, in a men's high-fashion boutique. He walked around the store, laughing at everything.

I stopped in front of the advanced underwear section. "New techniques!" the sign boasted. I picked up a package—it looked like a parody magazine cover for boardroom executives: blue shirt with white collar, power tie, no pants, underwear, soft focus, '90s textured backdrop. Inside was a pillowcase.

Eldon and I walked to a coffee shop that was actually a plane. "You flew to SF just to go to the SF airport?" the male flight attendant asked.

"Yeah shut up," I said, taking my now-familiar rearward-facing seat.

I landed in Portland and went to my apartment I forgot I had and ran into a long-lost roommate, Lazaro, swaddled in blankets. "You came back?" he said.

"Yeah shut up," I said.

Stephen showed up later but Laz plopped down on the loveseat next to him before I could. I found some old weed and a pipe in a rickety IKEA table, took a few hits, and passed the pipe to Laz. He emptied the pipe and reloaded it with something too dark to be weed.

Letting out the smoke with a strangely musical sound, Laz told Stephen he was smoking mugwort, but I knew it was actually just mold. "It's really good for your heart," he said. I scoffed and walked outside through a sliding glass door.

My mom's family was having a birthday party in the backyard for my little cousin, Trapper, with balloons and banners and all the bullshit. The festivities were staged around an enormous tree—half the family sat on either side. Most everyone was drunk and wearing shorts. My mom ignored her siblings as someone raised a piñata.

Trapper was squatting on the ground in front of me in that way kids do. "I wanna watch some porn," he said.

"That's okay!" I said. "You're a kid—you can watch kiddie porn."

Everybody laughed or froze and I walked back inside, opened a door, and descended into a musty dungeon.

A plump kid looking like a young Sean Astin ran down to me. "It's like *The Hobbit*!" he yelled, shaking a torch.

"Naww shut up," I said.

I opened a mahogany door—a surprisingly clean door, considering it was a dungeon and all—and saw an immaculate dining room, maybe early 2000s, but before I could continue admiring the fine dining ware, a hurricane-force wind punched the door shut.

I continued down to the next door. Inside was a series of rusted platforms suspended over a long huge rectangular lake of green slime.

"So," I said, "this is Hell."

I stood on the uppermost platform; more people entered the room behind me and I recognized them one by one. "Hey, that's Fat Friend!" I said, waving to an exceptionally round guy. "And that's..." I started, furrowing my brow at a small androgynous kid wearing goggles on their head, but I could only remember Fat Friend's name.

"Come on!" he shouted, "you gotta win this!"

I took the lead and we all jumped from platform to platform, careful not to fall in the slime. Eventually I landed on a barrel floating in the slime—there was nowhere else to go.

"Shit!" Fat Friend shouted. "We're doomed."

I looked back at him and winked. "Naww I got this," I said.

I pulled out a remote-control toy monster truck, put on some VR goggles, and walked into a pixelated video game version of the Hell slimepit room.

"You gotta win this!" a blocky Fat Friend shouted.

"Yeah shut up," I said, "and lemme concentrate."

I drove the truck around the room, jumping or using power-ups to teleport from platform to platform, but I still couldn't escape. There was one enemy in the game: a large demon fused to a teleporting dumptruck. As I stood there dumbstruck and admiring the truck's enormous wheels, an idea came to me.

"Meh, why not," I said.

I drove the toy truck into the demon dumptruck and used a teleport power-up—and then I found myself inside a rustic cabin filled with bright white luxury items.

As I walked up to a futuristic desk, the door opened and a man came in; a blizzard roared outside. "So," the man said, shaking snow off his trenchcoat, "what'll it be?"

He looked like a 1950s salesman. "Whaddya mean?" I asked. He looked at me like I was a very special square-peg round-hole kinda idiot.

"What..." he drawled, "are...you gonna buy...for your office?"

I wasn't surprised to suddenly have an office, but I still needed a second to decide.

"Hang on," I said. I walked over to the futuristic desk and touched it—the white bioplastic shimmered, glowing transparent, and a price tag, in many billions of yen, appeared above. I took back my hand—the desk became solid again, the price tag disappeared.

"So, you're telling me..." I said slowly, "that Hell...is an office...in a cabin...in the snow?"

He nodded.

"And all you do in Hell is...buy furniture?"

He nodded again.

A tremor started deep in my belly, gradually shaking its way up through my ribs and rattling my teeth—I laughed.

"Nawww," I said. "Fuck this!"

And then I was back on the barrel in the slimepit. "Guys," I said, turning to my friends, "it's all fake! Hell is just a gameshow—look!" I pointed to a sturdy stainless steel platform high above all the rusty jumping platforms: a man with a camera and a man dressed so tastelessly he had to be a 1970s gameshow host stood there, slackjawed and waiting.

"Fuck it," I said, "I'm out!"

And then I was biking through a forested park, other male cyclists moving all around me. A steam train made its way up the middle of the road, and we pulled over to let it pass.

Birds chirped glorious chirps. The sun came out, warming our backs. And there were no men with bad fashion tastes—at last, we were united and moving in the same direction, all of us clad in spandex.

Achromatic
by Krystina Holford

The world is tinted purple

the sky's a shade of green

the landscape reflects hues

of colors I have never seen;

I walk as if I'm floating

on a bright and crisp rainbow

and when you float on toward me

I whisper things you'll never know.

In a world where nothing's black and white

and reality's surreal

inhibitions're broken down

and I tell you what I feel.

All lines are blurred and coated

in twisted shades of gray

and in this space you kiss me

but in this dream that stays.

BIOS

AJD
AJD is a human person who resides in Cascadia.

KUMMAM AL-MAADEED
Kummam Al-Maadeed is an author from Qatar, who believes in magic and the existence of fairy worlds. She started writing in 2007 when she was attending Qatar University to study Mass Communications. She now works at Qatar University as a Section Head of Media & Publications, as she dreams about her next novel. *The Lost Rose* is her debut best selling novel. The first book of her new series, *Calling Magic*, is now available on Amazon.

ANDY ANDERSON
With a mix of authentic vulnerability, relevant truth, and humor, Andy Anderson writes poems that immediately make you want to be their friend. They are a co-organizer of Byrony Blaze's Queer Poetry Takeover in Portland, OR.

MICKEY COLLINS
~~Mickey rights wrongs. Mickey wrongs rites.~~ Mickey writes words, sometimes wrong words but he tries to get it write.

ALEXANDER DEMITRUS
Living in China, English books can be hard to come by. In a country that is known for being so dedicated to studying and education, books are highly revered. It has been my pleasure to bring some texts into China's library and build upon the bridge of knowledge between my home country and my current home.

MICHAEL FERAL
Michael Feral is a collector of rare books with a half-degree library science. He currently resides in Wimberley, Florida. He spends his time traveling, professionally, to Chongqing, China and back, as a sales representative for Wimberley Blinds and Shutters. This is Michael's first published translation.

L. FID
L. Fid is a member of a pseudonymous arts collective dedicated to world domination.

Desmond Everest Fuller

My name is Desmond Everest Fuller. My fiction has appeared in Rasasvada Creative and the Gorge Literary Review. I live and work in Portland, Oregon. I did work for years off and on in the fantastic bookstore, Artifacts: Good Books and Bad Art in Hood River, Oregon.

Krystina Halford

Krystina Holford formerly assisted in the maintenance of an educational library in Nanjing, China and guided in the sales of a spiritual library in Lake Forest, California. Now she can be found writing poetry, scripts, and an occasional short story if the mood strikes. Her greatest struggle in life is convincing herself to write instead of re-watch episodes of 'The Office", and she can't walk past a book store without touching at least one of the books inside.

Ryan Hall

Ryan Hall was born in Ogden, Utah, a place that holds the distinction of being where Hal Ashby grew up. He currently lives in Portland, Oregon with his wife and a cat, where he works at a bookstore.

Dan Heise

Dan Heise is an actor and writer originally from St. Louis, now living in Portland. He occasionally works at Powell's City of Books. He enjoys reading plays and young adult novels, and enjoys writing plays and poems. Dan discovered that he dreams more vividly when he drinks Pepsi. Somehow, he rarely dreams about Lord of the Rings or puns.

Ula Jankowska

Ula Jankowska, in some cities known as Miss Bookseller, is interested in books and people. Never leaves home without at least three books in her bag. Used to work as a bookseller for around 14 years now, in Warsaw, Wroclaw and Cracow. Now she is starting her own bookshop project in Prague. If you ask her to name three favourite writers, she will still name more and between these names will show up Italo Calvino, Jorge Louis Borges, Bohumil Hrabal, Ota Pavel, Tove Jansson.

Ariel Kusby

Ariel Kusby is a writer and bookseller based in Portland, Oregon. She currently works in the Rose and Orange rooms at Powell's City of Books, where she pays special attention to children's books about witches, odd cookbooks, and gnome gardening guides. You can check out her writing at www.arielkusby.com.

Ryan Shane Lopez
Ryan Shane Lopez is a teaching assistant and MFA fiction student at Texas State University, but previously worked as a bookseller for over two years. His fiction has been published in *Obra*, *Door Is a Jar*, and *Hypnopomp* magazines, and is forthcoming in *Abstract*. He has a wife, Hannah, and a three-year-old daughter, Josephine.

Leanna Moxley
Leanna Moxley spends most of her time wandering in and out of fictional dimensions, often guiding others through these portals in her work as a Powell's bookseller, and sometimes as a college writing teacher.

Elizabeth Neal
Elizabeth Neal is a Portland actress and bookseller. She is proud of her Union, ILWU Local 5.

Oaktea
Oaktea has always been in love with every aspect of a book--from the design to its contents, everything contributes to the experience. She started making comics for the all-in-one art and words combination, and eventually started working in bookstores to feed her voracious habit, as well as her love and respect for the form of the book itself.

Timothy Arliss Obrien
I am an interdisciplinary artist in music composition, writing, and visual arts. My goal is to connect people to accessible new music that showcases virtuosic abilities without losing touch of authentic emotions. I have premiered music with The Astoria Music Festival, Cascadia Composers, and Sound of Late's 48 hour Composition Competition. I also want to produce writing that connects the reader to themselves in a way that promotes wonder and self realization. I have self published several novels, and have written for Look Up Records (Seattle), Our Bible App, and Deep Overstock: The Bookseller's Journal. Check out my full discography, Where Are WE?, Piano Memories, Fear Sides and Soundbath, and my newest novel, *Dear God I'm a Faggot* at my website: www.timothyarlissobrien.com

Spencer Pond
Spencer Pond is a non-binary femme who is a film photographer and a writer. They have taking photos since they were 17 and found joy in poetry while Working at Food for Thought Cafe while studying at PSU. They co-curate the bi-yearly Persistent Existence benefit and previously were a curator and host of the Poetry Confluence readings.

Carole Reichstein
Carole works as a bookseller at Powell's.

Kevin Sampsell
Kevin Sampsell has worked at Powell's Books since getting hired as
"temporary" holiday help in 1997. He's now an events coordinator and the
small press section curator. He also runs the long-running micro press,
Future Tense Books. Besides his published writing, he has also contributed
collage art to a number of publications and websites.

Mike Santiago
Michael Santiago is an aspiring author and current English teacher in
Nanjing, China. He decided to get into education so that he could not only
travel the world doing what he loves, but to ignite that creative spark by
putting the power of storytelling into the hands of his students. His creative
drive and passion for literature has helped him translate the power of books
and their capacity to bestow knowledge onto his children.

Ben Talley
Ben Talley was raised in the humid stew of Alabama and is a pretty okay guy,
despite what the cat thinks. If you speak to his grandmother, let her know
that he eats regularly.

Jonathan van Belle
Jonathan van Belle is a bookseller at Powell's. He's the author of three books,
including the pre-posthumously published *Charter Party Companion
to Private Holidays* (all available in the most spider-infested kudzu
undergrowth of Amazon). At the moment, Jonathan is working to build
a philosophical community in Portland, with the aim of establishing a
permanent residence for the *Portland Philosophy Museum.*

Z.B. Wagman
ZB Wagman has always been able to find dreams tucked in the leaves of
books and squirreled away on the shelves of libraries and bookstores. He
recently started helping others find their dreams at the Beaverton City
Library.

Geoff Wallace
Geoff Wallace is a 55-year-old trapped in the body of an 18-year-old. His
twin selves are at work on many projects at once. He likes shelving picture
books at Powell's in Portland, Oregon.

Nicholas Yandell

Nicholas Yandell is a composer, who sometimes creates with words instead of sound. In those cases, he usually ends up with fiction and occasionally poetry. He also paints and draws, and often all these activities become combined, because they're really not all that different from each other, and it's all just art right?

When not working on creative projects, Nick works as a bookseller at Powell's Books in Portland, Oregon, where he enjoys being surrounded by a wealth of knowledge, as well as working and interacting with creatively stimulating people. He has a website where he displays his creations; it's nicholasyandell.com. Check it out!